Christm Whispers

A Wholesome, Small Town, Holiday Romance
Jada Stone

Contents

1.

2.

3.

4.

5.

6.

7.

8.

9.

10.

11.

12.

13.

14.

15.

16.

17.

18.

Chapter One

"He broke up with me!"

Ava's eyes flew wide as Beth flung herself across the table, her papers scattering, flinging her head down onto her arms as she sobbed.

"Max broke up with you?" Ava asked in disbelief.

Beth's shoulders shook, and she didn't answer. Biting her lip, Ava waited for her colleague to stop sniffling, readying a tissue in her hand.

"Can you believe it?" Beth's muffled voice came from somewhere between her arms and the table, and she was unsure what else to do. Ava reached across to squeeze her shoulder. Beth and Max had been steady for a while now, even though it had been a long-distance relationship since Beth worked here in the city and he was in some small town. However they'd worked it, it seemed to be going great, with Beth going away almost every other weekend. So Ava sure hadn't expected her to come back from visiting him with this news. Instead, she'd figured the opposite, sure that Beth would return with a ring on her finger and a smile on her face.

It looks like I got that wrong.

"I can't believe he'd do this to me – to us!"

Ava's lips twisted. "I'm so sorry, Beth. What happened?"

Still sniffling, Beth finally lifted her head, and Ava was able to hand her the tissue. Beth dabbed it at her eyes and then blew her nose. Her face was pale; her eyes were red, and tears stained her cheeks. Ava's heart went out to her.

"Max said I wasn't the person he thought I was. I told him that didn't make sense, but he didn't seem to care. He said... he said his life would be better without me."

"That's crazy!" Reaching across the table, Ava squeezed Beth's fingers. Her hand was so cold. "You guys have been going out for a while now. How could he say that he doesn't know you?"

Beth shrugged, her eyes still damp as she dropped her head again, her shoulders lifting slightly.

This is obviously still really painful for her. I shouldn't be asking her all these questions. She doesn't need that right now.

"I… I'm sorry, Beth. This has hurt you and –"

Beth waved a hand, her eyes closing tightly. "It's okay, Ava. I want you to know. I *want* to talk about this." She dragged in a shaking breath. "The truth is, I don't know what he means, but I can guess." Opening her eyes, tears still clinging to her lashes, she let out a slow sigh. "Max just wants to be free. There's plenty of pretty girls in Spring Forest."

Ava's mouth fell open, but Beth only nodded slowly, as if confirming what Ava thought was precisely what she meant.

"You think you he just pretended to want to be exclusive?"

Beth nodded, her brown eyes filling with tears again. Her lips pressed together, but there was a slight tremble that Ava couldn't help but notice. Her gut twisted, anger bubbling like lava in the pit of her stomach. Ava had never met Max – she and Beth weren't exactly close friends – but she knew how much time and energy Beth had put into her relationship these last few months. Ava didn't think that she'd ever seen Beth happier. Max had been all she'd talked about, to the point that she felt she *knew* him.

"I can't believe he did this to you. This probably isn't what you want to hear, but you don't need him." Then, speaking firmly, she grabbed Beth's hand and squeezed her fingers tightly. "You're better off without that guy. It would be best if you had someone who would commit to you and wants the same things. If Max thinks he can do better with some small-town girl from Spring Forest, let him find her. He'll learn soon enough that he should never have given you up, and by that time, it'll be too late."

Bet gave her a slightly sad smile although, to Ava's relief, she'd managed to stop crying. "You're the best, Ava. You're the first person I've told, and I knew you were the one to talk to." She sniffed, beginning to shred the damp tissue in her hand. "It only happened yesterday before I headed back into the city, and I've just been holding it in all morning." Then, flinging up one hand towards her red and now slightly swollen eyes, she shot a wry look towards Ava. "I just don't know what I'm going to do."

Determined, Ava thumped one fist down lightly on the table. "I'll tell you what you're going to do," she replied, as Beth jumped slightly. "You're going to forget about Max. You and I are going to get dressed up, and we're going to go out tonight - not so that you can meet someone new, but because you need to have some fun. Good food, good wine, and good company." Grinning, she let go of Beth's hand. "And you can complain about Max all you like, and I promise I'll listen to every single word." She and Beth hadn't gone out much before – but right now, this was something Ava figured Beth needed.

The remnants of the soggy tissue in Beth's hand didn't do much to wipe away her fresh tears, so Beth dabbed her eyes with the edge of her sleeve instead. "You are something, Ava. I don't think I deserve a friend like you."

Ava let out a soft exclamation. "Sure you do – and you'd do something like that for me too, I'm sure. If someone broke up with me, you'd probably already have at least five guys lined up outside to take me on a date."

"You mean you don't plan on doing that?" A tiny teasing smile was on Beth's lips, and Ava breathed a slow breath of relief. It looked like her friend was slowly coming back to herself. It wasn't like Beth to cry and certainly not to sob all over Ava right in the middle of the break room.

What an idiot he is to break up with someone like her.

"What'll it take to cheer you up?"

Beth's eyes suddenly shifted, flitting from one side of the room to the other as she caught her bottom lip between her teeth. Ava tipped her head, one eyebrow arching. She'd seen this expression on Beth's face before and knew exactly what it meant.

"Out with it."

Immediately, Beth's gaze went to Ava's face. Her mouth opened, forming a small circle, and she threw up both hands. "What are you talking about?"

"You know what I'm talking about." Ava began to smile; despite the fact, she was trying to keep her serious expression. "Whenever you do that, I know you've got something you want to tell me. You're just not sure if I'm going to say yes."

A heavy breath ripped from Beth's lips. She coupled her hands and rested them on her forehead, her elbows on the table as another breath blew out towards Ava.

"The thing is, I've got this Christmas book club conference coming up in a few weeks."

Ava nodded slowly, her smile suddenly dissolving. The Christmas conference was one that the publishing company they worked for – Golden Book Publishing – threw every year. It was always in various locations with different authors that the company represented, but it was one of the year's most popular events.

"Yeah, I remember." It wasn't a surprise that this was coming up. After all, Beth was the conference coordinator, and Ava was the publishing coordinator, so they sometimes had to work on stuff like this together. "What about it?"

Beth glanced up at her. There was a flicker of guilt dancing in her brown eyes. "Do you remember where it is?"

A little confused. Ava shook her head.

"It's at Spring Forest."

"Spring Forest?"

"Yeah, you know…" Dropping her hands to the table, Beth held Ava's gaze as though she ought to understand immediately that this was a big deal. But, instead, Ava stared back at her, searching through her memory for the reason that Spring Forest ought to stick in her mind, only for it to immediately come slamming back into her thoughts. Her eyes widened, and Beth nodded slowly, then rolled her eyes.

"Okay, so I admit I was a bit selfish in getting the conference at Spring Forest. In all honesty, it's this gorgeous little town, and I thought it would be magical at Christmas time –"

"And the fact that Max lives there wouldn't hurt," Ava finished as misery seemed to stick itself into every part of Beth's features. Her eyes filled, her face went pale, and she stuck her hands through her dark brown hair, letting out a small groan of frustration.

"I didn't think that we would break up; otherwise, I would *never* have it have had it in Spring Forest. But, now it looks like I'm going to have to go to the same small town where my ex-boyfriend lives and try to pretend everything's okay."

"But you won't see him, will you?" A little confused, Ava ran her fingers over her forehead. "I mean, I know it's a small town, but I can't be *that* small, Not if you were planning on throwing the conference there."

She wants me to go instead.

Butterflies immediately began to pour into Ava's stomach. Beth hadn't asked her yet, but she just knew in her gut that it was coming.

I understand that, though. If someone broke up with me, I'd be heading to the other side of the U.S. to get away from him.

"I'm not sure I could run the whole event for you." Then, deciding to be honest, Ava sat forward in her chair as Beth began to blink rapidly, her eyes a little glassy. "I get that you don't want to be in the same place as Max, but I'm not sure I'm the right person for this role."

Mainly because that's your job, and I'm not the one involved in running this thing. Not to mention Christmas is my favorite time of year. Who wants to work?

"We can't let down our clients, but I don't think I can do this." Reaching across the table, Beth grabbed Ava's hand. "I get that it's a big thing for me to ask you to do, but you've still got six weeks. I'll tell you everything there is to know about it, and I'll be only a phone call away if anything goes wrong. Plus, I'll clear it with everyone. It's

6

nothing more than introducing events and ensuring everyone turns up. If there are any problems, you can call me, and I'll be able to smooth them over right from this office."

"Still I –"

"I would appreciate this." Beth chewed her lip for a second, looking away, and her voice was quiet when she spoke. "I'm being honest, Ava. I don't think it's something I can do. Management won't understand, and I just –"

Tears were beginning to pool in the corners of Beth's eyes, and Ava found herself answering before she knew what she was saying. "You're right, and I'm sure it's something I can do. And like you said, I can call you anytime."

Immediately, doubts began to fling themselves at her, screaming at her to take back what she'd just said, but it was too late. Beth was crying again, but this time she was smiling.

"You've got no idea what this means to me. I'm so grateful. Thank you so much."

"That – that's okay." Her throat seemed to clog as Beth talked about just how much of a relief this all was and how much she owed Ava. Ava licked her lips, then reached for her glass of water to take a sip. Something inside her told her that this was a bad idea, but it was far too late. She couldn't back down, not now. It would ruin everything between her and Beth, probably shatter their new friendship, and she couldn't bring herself to do that. Beth had already suffered enough.

She took in a deep breath, set her shoulders, and tried to smile.

It   looks   like   I'm   going   to   Spring   Forest.

Chapter Two

For some reason, a constant beeping insisted on prodding Max out of a delicious dream. Groaning loudly, he grabbed his pillow, pulled it over his head, and pressed it down over his ears. Was that one of the neighbor's car alarms? Why haven't they gotten out of the house already to turn it off?

A loud whine managed to sneak its way past the pillow and into his ears, and Max responded by immediately throwing the pillow at the door. "Go back to bed, Baxter."

Max's head dropped into the pillow-free mattress, and he groaned. This was not the way he wanted to start the day.

The beeping didn't stop.

Pushing himself up on his elbows, Max forced his eyes open and looked around the room, trying to figure out where the noise was coming from.

And then his eyes landed on the alarm clock. The *new* alarm clock that he'd bought yesterday. The alarm was meant to get him out of bed on time, but right now, given the time on the clock, it looked like it had been going off for at least forty minutes.

Which meant he was going to be late.

"No, no, no, no, no!" A growl ripped from his throat as he threw back the sheet and practically ran for the door. Did he have time for a shower? Another glance at the clock told him there was no way he could manage it. But, if he got dressed and left right away, he might just make it on time. Otherwise, it looked like he was going to be late…again.

Not the best look for the Liberty Hotel's head chef.

Throwing open the bedroom door, he stumbled out, practically tripping over Baxter. When he finally caught himself, he had fallen into something mushy and warm.

Baxter howled.

Oh no.

Baxter had been expecting his breakfast, and it had been too tempting to go into the trash while he waited. He'd found something to eat, but it hadn't lasted in his stomach for all that long. Max's foot was now right in the middle of it.

Max let out a slow breath, closing his eyes, trying not to lose his temper as Baxter howled again.

"It's not your fault." Then, opening his eyes, Max scratched Baxter behind the ears while simultaneously pinching his nose with his other hand so he wouldn't smell whatever it was he was standing in.

It looks like I'll be going for that shower after all.

Twenty minutes later, with one happy, well-fed dog, Max tore out of his house and ran to his truck.

Shoving the key in the ignition, he revved the engine just as the light on the dashboard flickered on.

He needed gas.

This can't be happening.

Slamming his hand on the steering wheel, he let out a furious bark of frustration, then pushed the truck into gear. Living on the edge of Spring Forest had plenty of advantages but being on the opposite side of town from the gas station wasn't one of them. If he didn't get gas now, then he wouldn't have enough to get him back home after work - and he was working late tonight.

It doesn't look like I've got much choice.

Scowling, Max turned the truck toward the gas station, silently praying he had enough gas to get him there. Unfortunately, it looked like he was going to have a late start to the day, and that meant he was going to have to apologize to the boss for what was going to be the third time.

Good thing there aren't many good cooks around here. Otherwise, I might end up losing my job.

Taking a deep breath, Max tried to rearrange his expression. He wouldn't win any prizes for turning up to work with an attitude. Running one hand over his chin, his heart slammed against his chest.

He'd completely forgotten to shave.

Rubbing a hand on his face, Max sucked in his breath, forcing himself to push away the flood of frustration that burned red in the corners of his vision. Somehow, he was going to get through the rest of the day. All he had to do was get to the hotel.

Parking his truck was one thing Max had always been good at, but for whatever reason, it took him three attempts to reverse in between the lines. Max gritted his teeth as he tried again, muttering under his breath, finally managing to park straight. Then, grabbing his keys, he got out, slammed the door shut, and jogged toward the Liberty Hotel.

Rounding a corner, he bit back a muffled snarl of frustration when he practically collided with a young woman hauling her suitcase after her.

She turned to look at him, one eyebrow lifting as he stumbled back, both hands lifted, but his lips pulled back to bare his teeth.

This day just keeps getting worse and worse.

"Do you want to watch where you're going?"

10

Max blinked and put his hands on his hips.

It doesn't look like I'm about to get an apology, then. "Your suitcase nearly ran over my foot."

"That's hardly my fault." Piercing blue eyes gazed back into his as she flipped her blonde hair over her shoulder. She wasn't smiling. "You're the one who came barreling around that corner and almost ran straight into me."

"And you're the one who didn't watch where she was going!" he snapped back. He didn't have time to stand around any longer, protesting his innocence, and every second added to his lateness. Storming past her without a glance, he made his way directly into the hotel lobby, sidestepping various other guests. It wasn't his usual way of getting into work, but right now, he had to speak to Brandon. His friend would know whether the boss was on the warpath.

Moving around a crowd of guests that all seemed to want to check into the hotel simultaneously, Max caught Brandon's eye. Brandon always worked at the front desk, which was suitable for Max since it meant he knew exactly what was going on and precisely who to avoid when it came to the guests.

Brandon looked away, busy talking to one of the guests, and after a second, pointed to something they needed to sign before glancing back at Max. A quick lift of Max's eyebrow was all that was required for Brandon to understand the silent question. He gave a quick shake of his head, and Max closed his eyes in relief. It looked like the boss wasn't searching for him yet, which meant he'd gotten away with it so far.

What a relief.

Looking around at the vast number of guests, Max raised his eyebrows, wondering why it was so busy, only for his eyes to flare.

Of course. It's that conference.

In the craziness of the morning, he'd completely forgotten that it was the start of the Golden Book Publishing book club conference. It was a big deal, apparently. The publishing company represented some great authors, and this was the time for their fans to get to meet them. There would be discussions, book signings, and a lot of Christmas entertainment… which meant a ton of work for Max.

But today's silver lining is that Macy hasn't noticed I'm late. Turning on his heel, he quickly made his way toward the back stairs, grabbing his card key out of his pocket. As he walked, his eyes snagged on the same woman who had almost walked into him and tripped him up. She looked down at her cell phone, her lip caught between her teeth, and Max froze, his key card and work forgotten.

She looks really unsure about something.

Max's feet moved in her direction before he could stop himself, but he came up short, turning back around. After their last exchange, it wasn't like she would welcome his help like some damsel in distress. No doubt he'd just get another earful.

And I'm staying away from women, remember? He reminded himself. *Breaking up with Beth wasn't easy. The last thing I need right now is to be distracted by someone else. That would probably end badly, too.*

Letting a grimace settle over his features, Max headed to the kitchen.

Now that he thought about it, ever since he'd broken up with Beth, things had just seemed to get worse. Sleeping in late, never having any food in the refrigerator, and things like nearly running out of gas were happening far too often. He wasn't even looking *forward* to Christmas.

"What have we got?"

"You've got one sous chef about to hand in his notice."

At this remark, a dishcloth flew in Max's direction, thrown hard by the angry hand of Gordon. The man had never made head chef, and ever since Max was given the job two years ago, there had been a lot of tension between them. Max had never tried to resolve it, figuring it was Gordon's problem, but it looked like the man had had enough... and Max couldn't blame him. He had been scheduled to start the shift almost an hour ago, and Gordon had been forced to stay until he arrived. Dropping his head, Max balled his fingers into a fist in one hand, trying to keep his emotions in check. "This is completely my fault, Gordon. I'll go and talk to Macy. I'll tell her that –"

"No need to do anything like that." His jaw set, Gordon took one step closer to Max, his face red, his graying beard seeming suddenly whiter against the scarlet in his cheeks. "As I said, I've had enough of this place. I'll be handing in my notice, effective immediately. My wife's been begging me to move to the city, and it looks like I might take her up on that idea after all."

The whole kitchen went quiet as Max cleared his throat, unsure of what to say. If this was his fault, his doing, then no amount of apology was going to change Gordon's mind. "You – you'll get a great reference." Shrugging helplessly, he finally managed to look Gordon in the eye. "I know things haven't been great here the last month. I'm sorry about that."

Gordon shrugged. "Thanks, I guess."

"No problem."

Shaking his head, Gordon put one hand on Max's shoulder. "You need to step up." His voice was low, but still, shame burned over Max's skin. "You're head chef. Try and lead by example. I get that things have been tough for you lately, but you can't let that stop you from doing your job."

Max blinked, not sure what to say. There was a tightness in his throat that he couldn't get rid of, and he just couldn't look into Gordon's face for whatever reason.

Laughing lightly, Gordon dropped his hand and headed for the door. "Better warn you, Max," he said, his voice ringing around the kitchen. "With me gone, you'll *have* to get yourself here on time. Starting tomorrow."

Silence flooded the kitchen as Max licked his lips, caught between a laugh and embarrassment at Gordon's last comment. Swallowing hard, he looked around the kitchen, but everyone avoided his eyes.

Does everybody here know what happened between Beth and me?

Clearing his throat roughly, he threw up both hands, getting his head back into gear and his mind fixed on the job.

"So who's going to tell me what we've got going on? I know I'm late, and I'm sorry about that, but I'm here now, so someone will need to catch me up."

A line chef came over and began filling Max in on the details, leaving him with a clear picture of what they needed to prep for lunch and dinner. Max nodded, trying to take everything in, paying attention to his job and finding himself thinking about Gordon, about Beth, and about just how much of a mess his life was right now.

And it was all Beth's fault.

Chapter Three

Walking into her room, Ava didn't spend even a second looking around. Instead, she dropped her bag to the floor, let go of her heavy suitcase, and turned around to flop back onto the huge bed. Her eyes closed and she let out a long sigh.

Finally, I made it.

She had made it to Spring Forest without any trouble, but the journey had been longer and a little more uncomfortable than she'd expected. The airport was a bit farther out of town than she'd thought, but there had been a bus to take her into Spring Forest. A bus that had been crowded, hot, and smelly and had left her feeling pretty sick. It had been a huge relief to step out into the cold, crisp winter day, and she'd gulped the fresh air, looking all around her as she took in the Christmas decorations that adorned the front of the hotel. Someone had told her that there were loads more decorations in town, and she planned to walk through it at some point, but right now, all she wanted to do was sleep.

That guy didn't help.

Her nose wrinkled as she thought about him. He'd practically snarled at her, his dark eyes narrowing when she'd shot right back at him that it hadn't been her fault. A small smile crossed her lips.

Maybe he hadn't expected that.

Closing her eyes, she flopped one hand over them. Yes, he'd been rude, but she hadn't been able to stop herself from noticing how broad his shoulders were and how tightly his white T-shirt had clung to her arms – even when he'd been scowling at her. His black hair was messy, though, as if he'd shoved both hands through a couple of times. Idly, she wondered what he would look like if he actually smiled, and then quickly threw that thought away.

Don't need to give him even a second of thought. I probably won't see him again.

Her hand flopped back to the bed.

Unless he's here as one of the guests.

Ava's eyes flew open.

Or worse, one of the authors.

Her heart began to pound furiously as she fought to remember the five authors that were coming for this week-long event. Later this evening, she would have a brief meet and greet with each one of them, where they would go over the program and make sure that everybody was happy with what was happening. Tomorrow would kick off the event, and based on the huge crowd of guests that arrived at the same time as her, Ava was pretty sure most of them were here for the conference. The Book Club conference was always a popular event, and fans came from all over the country to be part of it. Spring Forest seemed like a quaint, quiet little place, and the sheer number of visitors might be something of a shock for the quiet little town.

Squeezing her eyes closed again, Ava tried to remember each of the authors' names. She knew there were three women and two men, but no matter how hard she tried, she couldn't remember what they looked like. If that guy who had practically run into her was one of the authors, Ava didn't know what she was going to do. That would already be a really bad first impression.

Her cell rang, and Ava grabbed at it. "Hello?"

"Ava? How is it all going? Did you make it to Spring Forest okay?"

At the sound of Beth's voice, Ava let out a huge sigh of relief, prompting Beth to begin to ask a million questions, obviously afraid that something had already gone wrong.

"Calm down, Beth." Laughing, Ava pushed herself up to sit. "I'm totally fine. I got here, no problem. I just got checked in." Thinking it was probably best not to talk about the guy she'd bumped into, Ava let out another audible breath of relief. "I guess I'm just glad to be here. These past few weeks have been crazy."

"Which is why I'm so grateful for you taking this on for me." Beth's voice was warm and filled with an appreciation that Ava knew she could trust. "It really has meant a lot to me."

"It's no trouble." Ava got up from the edge of the bed and wandered into the bathroom, rolling her eyes at the dark shadows that hung under her eyes. "I'm just going to unpack, grab a coffee and then go meet these authors." Licking her lips, she wondered whether to ask Beth about them.

It would put my mind at rest, at least.

"Remind me how old they all are…"

"How old are they?" Beth repeated, sounding confused. "Why? What's that have anything to do with it?"

"Well, I can't remember their faces, even though you've shown me their pictures a few times," Ava admitted as Beth laughed. "I figure if you just tell me how old they are, then I'll know who I can look for."

"Or you could just look at the document I've just sent you." Beth giggled at Ava's exclamation. Putting her cell phone on speaker, she opened up her e-mail. "I've sent you a photo of each of them, so that should help."

Ava said nothing, scrolling quickly down the page as she looked first at the three women and then at the two men. To her relief, none of them was the guy she'd argued with earlier that day. Her eyes closed as she smiled.

What a relief.

"This is great. Thanks, Beth. And yes, before you ask, I've read all the books you suggested, so I know exactly what they'll be talking about!"

Beth laughed again. "That's great – and it's no problem. That's what I do, and right now, I'll do anything to help you since you've been so generous in stepping into my place."

Ava shrugged. "It really is okay. I'm sure the conference is going to be great, and I'm looking forward to it, actually." *At least I am now that I know that guy isn't going to be there.*

"I'll check in with you regularly." Beth's voice had taken on a slightly more official tone. "And call me anytime with anything."

Ava nodded, even though she knew Beth couldn't see her. "Absolutely, I will."

"Oh, and remember that Danielle Phillips – she's the one at the top of your document – has a specific food allergy. I think it's very severe because she carries an EpiPen with her at all times. I've already doublechecked this with the catering team, but it would probably be best to make certain that they know for sure not to give her anything with… what was it again?"

"Nothing with eggs." A small frown creased Ava's forehead. "That's a good idea. I'll go check to make sure the caterers know about it. That's a pretty big deal."

"It sure is." There was no hint of laughter in Beth's voice, the serious tone still lingering as they talked business. "We want to make sure our authors are well looked after and that the fans have the best experience too so they keep coming back year after year."

A heavy mantle of responsibility fell on Ava's shoulders. "I won't let you down," she promised firmly. "I'd better get going. I still have to put away my things, shower, and change before I go meet the authors."

"And get yourself that cup of coffee." Beth's teasing laughter filled her voice again, now that they weren't talking about the conference. "I don't believe for a second you'll let me down, either. You'll have a great time tonight, for sure. Call me tomorrow, okay?"

"I will," Ava promised before the call ended.

Setting her cell down on the desk at one end of the room, she finally took in her surroundings, taking a few moments to try to release some of the tension that Beth had put onto her shoulders with a reminder about just how much she was responsible for this weekend.

I can do this.

Making her way across the room, Ava turned on the coffee pot, then set about unpacking her things. Yes, there was a lot to do, and yes, she had to oversee pretty much everything this weekend, but she could do it.

If Beth can do it, there's no reason why I can't. Plus, this will look great on my resume when the time comes for me to move on from Golden Book Publishing.

It took her longer than she thought to put away all of her things. By the time she'd showered, changed, and taken one sip of her coffee, it was time to head down to meet the authors. Pulling her mouth to one side, Ava gave herself a long look in the bathroom mirror. She'd barely had time to properly do her hair – which wasn't exactly going to be the best look, not when she was representing the company. Her dirty blonde hair hung a little more limply around her shoulders than it had this morning even though she'd washed it, and there were definite heavy shadows under her eyes. Grabbing her makeup bag and praying she wouldn't be late, she spent a few minutes tying her damp hair back into a messy bun, adding some foundation and a touch of lipstick which made her look – and feel – a whole lot better. With a smile that held more confidence than she felt, Ava turned around to head for the door.

It was time to start the book club conference.

"Thank you all so much for coming this week. I know it's going to be a great success." Ava's cheeks ached as she forced herself to hold the smile she'd placed there at the very start of her meet and greet. The five authors all smiled back at her, and Ava couldn't help but go over their names and their genres silently in her head for the sixteenth time.

Danielle Philips (romantic comedy), Taylen Ingram (fantasy), Lucinda Richards (crime thrillers), Clayton Scott (horror), and Lance Vinson (science fiction). Yes, I know them all.

Ava shook their hands one after the other, wishing each one a good night as they all headed up to their rooms. It had taken longer than Ava had expected to have that meeting, and she was completely exhausted.

I don't feel like I have enough energy to climb the stairs back to my room. She sighed. *Wait. Have I eaten today?*

"Excuse me?" Shifting in her chair, she waved one hand at someone who looked as though he worked at the hotel.

"Yes?"

Ava eyed his name badge. "Brandon? I'm Ava. I'm one of the guests here."

Brandon nodded his head, with a gentle smile on his face and soft green eyes holding her gaze. She put him as a little older than her, maybe mid-to-late thirties, with short-cropped dark hair that was graying at the temples. "Yes, I remember. I checked you in earlier today."

Ava's eyes widened. "Oh. Right. Yes, sure. Was that you?" Waving one hand, she shook her head and pulled her gaze away, a little embarrassed. "Sorry, it's been a long day."

"And from the look of it, you haven't eaten."

Surprised, Ava narrowed her gaze slightly, only for Brandon to grin and gesture to the five empty plates with cutlery strewn across them – and then to Ava's place, which was completely clear of dishes. A flash of awareness hit her.

"Oh, right. Yes, exactly. I know it's super late, but is there any chance that I could get something to eat? I'll take anything, even if it's just a muffin or something. Even a banana!"

"I know for a fact that the head chef is working late tonight." Brandon smiled sympathetically. "Why don't I call him and see if he can rustle something up for you?"

Ava had to stop herself from grabbing his hand to stay thanks, her stomach growling furiously at the very same time. Her flush deepened. "Sorry about that."

Brandon laughed. "Don't worry about that. My wife's stomach rumbles if she even so much as *looks* at a donut. You must be really hungry. I'll get something here for you in just a few minutes."

Suddenly remembering what Beth had told her, Ava quickly caught Brandon's attention again before he could leave. "Wait a second. Could I speak to this head chef of yours? It's about the conference. One of the authors has a specific allergy, and I want to make sure the kitchen knows about it."

Brandon nodded. "Sure, that's no problem. I'll get him to bring up whatever it is he can make you himself. Do *you* have any allergies I should know about?"

Ava shook her head. "No. Thank you very much. I appreciate this."

"All part of the service." Brandon shrugged. "It's what you get in a small town like Spring Forest. This is what we call small-town hospitality."

"Well, I really appreciate it." Giving Brandon a quick smile, Ava sat back in her chair and closed her eyes as a sigh broke from her lips. Every part of her wanted to just sink into the chair. She was so tired.

At least the meeting with the authors went well, and I know what I'm doing tomorrow. I'm sure it's going to be great.

She glanced at her cell phone, but the screen was dark. *And Beth's on the other end of the line if I need her.*

"Hi there, you must be Ava. I've made you some –"

Ava glanced up at the chef as he set the tray on her table, wondering why he'd trailed off like that, only for her breath to swirl in her chest. Her eyes grew fixed as she stared at the very same man who had been so rude to her earlier. The man who'd accused her of running him over with her suitcase when *he* had been the one who had come barreling around the corner without even thinking about who might be in his path.

"It's… it's you."

The man cleared his throat and then tucked his hands behind his back. He looked a little better than before, Ava had to admit. His hair wasn't so crazy, but there was still that scruff about his face – which Ava had to admit wasn't exactly a bad thing. With a square-cut jaw, a roman nose, and dark brown eyes, there was something brooding about him – but Ava wasn't about to let herself get distracted. Not right now.

"You're the head chef, then, huh?"

Her eyes drifted down over his once-white double-breasted jacket, which was covered in stains – the sign of a hard day's work, she figured, and whatever he'd set down smelled delicious. But that didn't mean that she was exactly pleased to see him.

A brash cough broke from him. "Yes. I'm the head chef here."

"Right." She searched his shirt for a name badge, but there wasn't one. Frowning, she quickly realized he wouldn't need one. He said he was always in the kitchen and not up front with the guests like Brandon was.

"Brandon said you were hungry." He gestured with his chin to the tray. "As I was saying, I've put decaf coffee out for you given the hour. And there's lots of fresh orange juice there for you, and this is lasagna with some garlic bread on the side."

Ava blinked. His tone was so different now that he knew she was one of the guests here, but that tightness about his mouth was still there, and he didn't seem able to look into her eyes. Was he embarrassed? Or was this just how he was?

"Thank you."

"It's no problem," he said without a smile, and he turned away only for Ava to reach out to grab the edge of his sleeve. "Hang on a second, please." She dropped his sleeve immediately, but not before her fingers brushed his as he turned back to face her.

"I had another thing I wanted to ask you." Ignoring the quickened thrum of her heart, Ava lifted her chin slightly as she looked up at him. "I'm coordinating the Golden Book Publishing book club conference this year. As you may know, we're running it in this hotel."

The chef didn't say anything, but his jaw tightened a little as he looked away from her. Ava's stomach twisted. Was there something about this conference that he didn't like?

Pushing that worry aside, she got straight to the point. "One of our authors, Danielle, has a very specific egg allergy. I believe she has an EpiPen, given the severity. I wanted to make sure that the kitchen is aware of that and won't serve her anything containing eggs."

The chef nodded. "Yes, we have been told about Ms. Phillips' allergy." He answered quickly. "Is that everything?"

Wrestling against the urge to throw something back at him given the sharpness of his reply, Ava closed her mouth tight again and then shook her head. There wouldn't be any good reason to speak with him. It wasn't like she would see him often since he would be in the kitchen and she would be running the conference. They weren't exactly going to become friends.

"No, I don't think so. I don't think there's anything else." He went to turn away, but Ava held up one hand, turning her attention back to the lasagna. "But I sure would like some dessert. If you could bring it up in, let's say, thirty minutes, I would really appreciate it."

One glance told her that his expression had darkened even more, but Ava didn't care. In fact, she found herself smiling. "Thank you so much."

Turning her attention back to the lasagna, she picked up her fork and put the first forkful into her mouth. Sure, it was a bit petty to make him stay at work for a little longer just to bring her dessert, but after the way he treated her today, she figured he deserved it.

And this was going to taste even sweeter because of it.

Chapter Four

"**I**'m awake!"

Grabbing his cell phone off the nightstand, Max tapped wildly at the screen, trying to find the button that would turn off his alarm. Managing to silence the rattling whistle, he set it back down, turned it over, and closed his eyes.

It felt like he'd only just rolled into bed. How could it be time for him to get up and get going again? He didn't even feel rested.

That's probably because I was at the hotel late last night – long after my shift – talking to Brandon about that woman.

Ava Patterson was the one running the book club conference at the hotel this week, which meant she was going to be around a whole lot. Not that it mattered to Max since he was able to stay down in the kitchen, just like he normally did. It wasn't in his job description to spend time with the guests.

His eyes opened as the overly cheerful tune from his cell phone alarm went off again. Letting out a yell of irritation, he sat up, grabbed it, and managed to turn it off. This was the fourth time he had to turn it off. What was wrong with his phone?

Forcing himself to sit up instead of collapsing back down onto the bed as he wanted, he found the clock icon, tapped it, and then stared at the multiple alarms that had been set. They were all one minute apart and went on for the next hour.

There was no way he'd done that. Yes, he'd set one or two, but –

Brandon.

Unable to stop the grin that spread across his face, Max ran one hand over his eyes, then let it trail down his face. He left his phone at the desk yesterday when he'd gone to get changed out of his chef's stuff – just after he'd finished complaining about Ava and telling Brandon all about his disastrous morning, starting with the fact that he'd just kept on sleeping through his alarm, no matter how much he tried.

Since Brandon knew his passcode, no doubt he'd set all of those alarms just to make sure Max got to work on time today.

Gotta admit it worked.

Forcing himself out of bed, Max wandered to the bedroom door and found Baxter sitting just outside. He lifted his head, hopefully, and Max bent down to scratch at the dog's ears.

"I know. Crazy, right? Looks like you're going to get walked *and* fed this morning."

The last few days, he'd asked his neighbor, Mrs. Williamson, to walk Baxter when Max was at work. She loved it, of course, otherwise, Max would never have considered asking. No doubt she'd come by later to walk Baxter again, but the dog would love the extra attention.

Taking a deep breath, Max set his shoulders and headed downstairs with Baxter at his heels. The first thing he was going to do was shower and shave. Then he'd walk Baxter, grab some breakfast, feed the dog, and head to work. Hopefully, he wouldn't run into Ava again – although, knowing his luck, that's exactly what would happen, and it would end up ruining his day.

***

"Good morning."

Max grinned as the sous chef, Heather, arched one eyebrow. She was married to Brandon, and they worked at the hotel together – practically keeping it together half the time, Max thought.

"You don't need to look so surprised. The number of alarms Brandon set, I'm surprised that I wasn't in here earlier."

Heather grinned. "Oh yeah, he told me he'd done that. I'm glad to see it worked!"

Max rolled his eyes, laughing. "It did more than work. I don't think I've ever been more awake first thing in the morning."

Grinning, Heather lifted both shoulders. "Then maybe you should keep them," she said softly, and as much as Max didn't want to admit it, it probably was a good idea.

"Yeah, I'm sorry about sleeping in and coming in late recently. Things haven't been great since... well, you know."

Heather nodded. "I do. Brandon hasn't told me a whole lot but did say it wasn't a good way for things to end."

That's an understatement.

"Yeah, it wasn't great." He gave her a wry smile, then shrugged as though it really didn't mean very much. It bothered him that he'd broken up with his long-term, long-distance girlfriend on the very same day that he'd planned on proposing.

Get your thoughts back on the job. Beth isn't part of your life anymore.

He cleared his throat. "The authors and the guests at the book club conference are going to eat in a separate dining room. Is that right?"

Heather nodded. "That's about right. We're using the large conference dining hall – the one we use when there are weddings and things."

Max grinned. "Makes things easier for us, right?"

Laughing, Heather shrugged. "Sure. I've got one team in one dining room and another team in the other, so we should be just fine."

"Sounds great. Before I forget, there's one guest who has a severe egg allergy." Looking around the kitchen, he called for everyone to give him their attention for a second. The last thing he wanted was to have one of the guests collapse from some horrific allergic reaction that they could have prevented. "I want everyone to make sure that they are listening right now. We have a guest on the premises with a severe egg allergy. Her name is Danielle Phillips. She is one of the authors at the book club conference, and under no circumstances is she *ever* to be given anything that contains egg."

"Yes, chef." The call rolled around the rooms, and Max nodded, choosing not to break into a smile. His team had to know how serious this was. "I want everything checked and double-checked before you serve it to her. As far as I know, none of the other guests have anything serious or anything we need to be aware of, aside from the usual vegan and vegetarian options. If anything more comes to light, I will let everyone know."

When he called for everyone to go back to work, Heather beckoned him over.

"Not to make things more difficult for you when we've got a really busy week coming up, but we really need to hire a new sous chef. It can't be just me. We've got enough to cover us for the next couple of days, and I can do extra, but we're not going to survive with people just picking up Gordon's slack."

Max blew out a breath, pinching the bridge of his nose for a second. "I totally forgot about that."

"That's why I'm here to remind you," Heather grinned as Max laughed.

"Right, thanks, Heather. I'll get on it."

Going across the kitchen to wash his hands, Max exhaled slowly. It felt like everything was piling on him – first with Beth and then with his issues being late for work, the fact that he forgot things, was barely sleeping – and when he did, sleeping for far too long – and now with this conference on top of it all.

"I'll just have to deal with it all," he muttered aloud to himself. Max gritted his teeth. This was Christmas time, and he was meant to be full of spirit, the joy of Christmas. He'd expected to love every day and had thought he'd be looking forward to spending Christmas Day with Beth, but now, he just felt empty, like he had nothing to look forward to and nothing to be hopeful about. As far as he was concerned, Christmas Day would pass like every other day – and maybe that was a good thing.

I'll offer to work Christmas Day. Let someone with a family have the day off.

Taking a deep breath, Max set his hands on the counter, dropped his head, and closed his eyes for a second. He had to get his thoughts off Beth and back on his work. Otherwise, this lunch would just add itself to the pile of growing disasters he was leaving in his wake.

***

"Well, we did it!"

Grabbing the hat off his head, Max flung it on the counter and then grinned back at Heather. Despite how he had been thinking and feeling earlier, the whole day went really well. The lunch had gone off without a hitch. The guests had commented on how good everything tasted – and dinner had gone just the same. All that was left now was to bring up tea and coffee and leave everybody else to clean up. He was at the end of his shift. He could go home, relax, and worry about tomorrow when it came.

"Brandon should be finished about now too," Heather continued from behind him. "You got anything else you want me to do? I could take up that coffee." She gestured to it, and Max turned around, his lips pursed. One of the servers should have brought that along already.

"No, don't worry about it, I'll do it. You go on." Unbuttoning his chef's coat, he chucked it next to his hat and then headed toward the door.

"Are you sure? I'm happy to do it, and it won't take me more than a few minutes."

"A few minutes that you could be spending with Brandon," Max replied with a smile. "It's no trouble. I'll see you tomorrow."

Heather gave him a warm smile. "I appreciate it. See you tomorrow, Max."

Heading through the double doors that would lead him out to the hallway, Max made his way straight to the private dining room. He didn't want to run into Ava again, but if it meant that Heather and Brandon could head home together, then he was happy to do this. All he had to do was hand in the tray of coffee and tell one of the servers to take it around to the remaining guests. *Then* he could go home.

The door was a little ajar, and Max carefully pushed his way inside. The room was quiet, which wasn't what he had expected. Catching the eye of one of the servers, he walked up to him and handed him the tray. He was about to make his way back toward the door when a voice caught his attention, and he found himself turning his head.

Ava was standing at the front of the room, a microphone in her hands and a bright smile on her face. Max had no idea what she was talking about, but it wasn't like he was paying any attention. Something had twisted tight in his chest, and try as he might, he couldn't seem to get his feet to move to the door. When Ava smiled, her face completely transformed.

She was absolutely gorgeous.

Her blonde hair was curled and fell gently around either side of her heart-shaped face. Her eyes were sparkling with laughter, and her cheeks were a gentle pink. She was looking one way and then the other as she spoke, talking about whatever it was with great and obvious passion, and, for a second, Max found himself wanting to sit down at one of the tables and just listen. He wanted to take her in, wanted to drink in the sight of her.

And then someone coughed, and the moment shattered around him. Shaking his head, he turned away, scrunching his eyebrows. The last thing he needed was to get distracted by someone like Ava. Sure, she was pretty, but she was only going to be here for the week, and he wasn't the sort of guy to have a fling.

And even if he wanted to start something with Ava, it's not like she'd say yes.

A wry smile dragged itself across his lips, but instead of opening and stepping out of the door, Max found himself leaning back against the wall, watching Ava out of the corner of his eye. Everybody laughed at something she said, and Max jerked slightly in surprise, heat rising his chest as though they were laughing at him. Telling himself he was being stupid, he turned his head so that he could look directly at Ava, just to make sure – only for their eyes to meet.

For a second, she paused. That smile began to drift away, and then it was back as she snapped her attention to someone else.

"And so that leads us to the end of day one." Ava's gentle voice filled the room through the microphone. "You are welcome to enjoy the many facilities the hotel has to offer for the remainder of the evening – and I'm sure one or two of our authors might come join you! Otherwise, I guess I'll see you bright and early at tomorrow morning's Book Panel session. Remember not to be late!"

As everyone applauded, Ava's eyes twisted back toward Max, and he caught himself looking straight back at her, unable to drag his eyes away. Her smile was gone, and as she set the microphone down, Max pushed away from the wall.

It's probably time to leave… unless…

Clearing his throat, he found himself glancing at her again. It was obvious she'd seen him here and wasn't exactly happy about it – but maybe he should do something about that.

I probably should apologize. I can admit I was in a bad mood, even if she did have a huge suitcase.

Shrugging to himself, he turned directly to face her, taking purposeful steps in her direction. She grimaced, only for that grimace to disappear when someone else spoke to her. Max watched with thinly veiled amusement as the smile she'd been able to wipe off so easily came straight back as she nodded, listened, and then gestured to the door to one of the guests.

Looks like she's as much in hospitality as I am.

"Tough crowd?"

Ava lifted her chin, her eyes sparkling with obvious dislike. "Is there something wrong?"

"No."

His heart suddenly began to slam itself against his ribs and he winced, absentmindedly rubbing at it as he tried to find a way to begin. "I – I was bringing up coffee."

Blinking, Ava said nothing, and Max dropped his head and ran one hand over the back of his neck.

This is not going well.

"I actually… " *Why is this so difficult?*

"If you're coming to apologize, then you are actually going to have to say those words." The ice in her tone sent a cold shiver down his spine, and he flung out both hands to either side.

"Yeah. That's what I was trying to do." Finally, he was able to hold her gaze and, to his relief, saw her shoulders drop. She wasn't going to ask him to go away, at least.

"I shouldn't have yelled at you like that. I was rude and blamed you for something that wasn't your fault," Max offered.

Her head tilted slightly. "And… ?"

Max hesitated. "And… and I don't want there to be any tension between us, not when we both have a job to do. I shouldn't have said or done any of that. I was in a bad mood, and I'd had a terrible morning – none of which is an excuse, by the way – but I shouldn't have taken it out on you."

Ava didn't immediately reply. Instead, she stuck her hands to her hips and let her eyes search his face as though she was trying to work out whether he was being honest with her. Max closed his eyes briefly, silently praying that she'd find what she was looking for.

"And you're not just saying this to try and make the hotel look good? If your apology is trying to get a better hotel satisfaction survey outta me, then-"

Max's eyes snapped open. "I swear to you. It's got nothing to do with that. I mean every word, I swear." The next second, he looked down and realized that his hand had gone to Ava's arm. When he looked back up at her, Ava's eyes had rounded a little, and then, after another second, she stepped back as Max dropped his hand. Completely embarrassed at what he'd inadvertently done, Max clasped his hands behind his back as if doing that would stop him from touching her again. His fingers were tingling for some reason, and something was buzzing around his head like a wasp. "I promise, this is just what it looks like. I realize I acted poorly, and I'm sorry."

Ava's eyes flashed away from him for a second, then she looked back, chewing the edge of her lip. "Okay. Thank you for that." A small smile tugged one side of her mouth as she shrugged her shoulders – the first glimpse of a smile Max had ever gotten from her. "I guess we all have bad days."

"Yeah, that was a real bad day for me." Letting out a slow breath of relief, he returned her smile. There was definitely still some tension between them, but to him, it wasn't from their argument the first day they'd met. This was something different, something he wasn't sure he wanted to explore. *It's probably best just to leave it there.* "I'd better let you get on. My shift's over, so I'll be heading home. If you ever want to see the town, though, all you've got to do is ask. Maybe I can make this up to you."

What am I saying? I don't want to take her out into Spring Forest... do I?

Resisting the urge to rub one hand over his face, Max turned around, about to head out of the room, only for Ava to catch his arm.

Again, the tingling sensation shot through him as he turned around to face her, wondering if she was about to take him up on the offer.

"I... I just realized that I don't know your name." Ava pressed her lips together, her eyes dancing around his face. "I'm guessing you know that I'm Ava – Ava Patterson."

Max smiled, trying to ignore the way his heart had suddenly gone from a slow beat to a furious hammering. "I sure do. Once I realized that you work for the Golden Book Publishing Company, it was easy enough to figure out who you were."

A slight flush rose in Ava's cheeks as her fingers twirled one long strand of dark blonde hair around and around, and Max's stomach tightened. As much as he didn't want to admit it, with that cute smile and those stunning blue eyes, she was gorgeous.

"And... ?" It wasn't until Ava lifted her eyebrow and grinned at him that Max realized she was waiting for him to introduce himself. Feeling the heat that climbed up his chest, Max cleared his throat roughly, then shoved both hands into his pockets, shrugging his shoulders. "I'm Max. As you know, the chef here at the Liberty Hotel. If you ever need something good cooked – or fireproofed – I'm the one to call."

Why did I have to say something like that? That sounded really dumb.

Ava immediately began to frown, and Max let out a small sigh. "Sorry about that. I just was trying to say – in a weird way – that I'm also one of the volunteer firefighters here in Spring Forest. That's all."

Ava frowned thoughtfully. "You said your name is Max." She was speaking a little more slowly now, her eyebrows lowering heavily over her eyes.

Max nodded. "Yeah, I did. Max Williams."

Without any obvious reason, Ava sucked in a sudden breath, her eyes growing wide. Then she took a small step back, wrapped her arms around her waist as though she were trying to protect herself from him, and shook her head. "Right. Max." She nodded her head to herself, turning away slightly. "I – I'd better go. There are a lot of things I have to see to, and I can't spend all my time talking to one of the hotel employees. I doubt we'll run into each other again."

Max blinked, the smile falling from his lips as he stared after Ava, seeing her walk a straight line away from him. Her steps were quick as if she couldn't wait to put as much distance between them as she could. Becoming more and more confused at her strange response to hearing his name, Max shoved one hand through his hair, his nose wrinkling as he followed her with his eyes.

What just happened?

Taking his hands out of his pockets, Max headed for the door, his forehead still furrowed. He had done what he came here to do, hadn't he? There wasn't another reason for him to hang about. Throwing one more glance in Ava's direction, he ambled toward the door and headed out. All he had to do was grab his stuff, and then he could get on home for the night. He'd already stayed around a whole lot later than he'd meant to.

Something buzzed in his pocket. Pulling out his cell phone, he glanced down at the message that had come through. It was from Brandon, reminding him about the Christmas party that he and Alice were throwing in a couple of days and wondering if he had anyone he wanted to bring.

Does Brandon seriously think I'd have a plus one right now?

Max's lopsided smile was a little sad as he typed a message back. For some reason, Ava was the only person that popped into his head, but he shook the thought away quickly enough. There was no way that he would *ever* ask Ava. Yes, she was gorgeous, but there was still something strange going on between them, and Max wasn't sure he wanted to find out what it was. He'd already had enough trouble with Beth. The last thing he wanted was to throw himself head over heels into something else.

Chapter Five

I *can't believe she didn't tell me.*

Pulling out her cell phone, Ava found Beth's number and pressed the call button. Her lungs were heaving, sucking in the air as she waited for Beth to pick up, the shock still running like lightning through her veins.

Great. Voicemail.

"Beth? You'd better call me the minute you get this." Taking in a breath, she closed her eyes. "Why didn't you tell me that your ex-boyfriend works here?"

Ending the call, she threw her cell phone into her bag and leaned back against the wall of the conference room as she attempted to focus.

I've got a job to do right now. I can panic about this later.

Sure, most of the guests were heading out into Spring Forest or to one of the various facilities the hotel had to offer, but that didn't mean she couldn't keep a smile on her face and answer questions any of the lingering guests had. *And* she had to make sure that the authors were happy with the plan for tomorrow and finish setting up the panel tables. Everything was going well with the conference, at least, and she couldn't let Max ruin things for her. It wasn't like they were going to be in the same room all that often, was it?

All the same, it's still awkward knowing that he's here. And I don't understand why Beth didn't warn me!

Taking in another long breath, Ava lifted her head. At least she knew now why Beth had been so desperate not to run the conference at this hotel. She would have definitely run into Max at some point, and Ava couldn't imagine how embarrassing, how difficult that would have been for her. Pressing her hands to her cheeks as if that could take away some of the heat, Ava closed her eyes and tried to push Max's grinning face out of her head. As much as she hated to admit it, Ava knew she'd been busy admiring Max only five minutes before he'd told her his name. His green eyes had been almost vivid, and she'd caught the gold flecks gleaming through them when he'd smiled. Ava had found herself imagining what it would be like to push her fingers through his thick brown hair, her gaze roving down over him and silently wondering just how easily he'd be able to lift her off the ground. Max was broad-shouldered, with a sense of strength practically emanating from him in every single movement he made. If she was honest, it had been easy to see him as a firefighter – but even now, that thought sent a shiver through her, and she quickly pushed it away. There is no way she could let herself have *any* sort of feelings for Beth's ex-boyfriend, especially after she knew how he broke her heart.

"What a great night."

Ava was a little startled as someone touched her shoulder, turning around to see Lucinda Richards, one of the authors, smiling at her. "Oh, thank you. I'm so glad you're enjoying the conference so far."

"We sure are. We're still meeting in the smaller conference room in thirty minutes, right?"

Ava nodded. "Right. I just need to make sure that everything is set up here, and then I'll be right with you all."

"Great." Lucinda gave her a broad smile before turning around and heading toward the door, catching up with the other authors.

Ava watched them go, letting out a slow breath and then gritting her teeth.

I have to get my mind off Max and back on this conference. I'm still going to have a word or two with Beth when she calls, though. That was a surprise, and not a good one. Tossing her head, Ava made her way to the front of the room, ready to get set up for the morning. *I just hope there's nothing else I don't know.*

"I take it you got my message then?"

"Ava, I'm so sorry." Beth practically wailed, beginning to beg for Ava's forgiveness. "I totally meant to tell you, but with everything that was going on, I guess I just forgot."

"Then Max *is* your ex-boyfriend, right?"

"Yes." A small sniffle followed the admission.

Ava closed her eyes. "You should have told me."

"I know I should have." Beth sniffled again, and Ava's heart bruised with the nudge of guilt. In bringing up Max, was she making Beth relive everything all over again? "Trying to get organized for the conference was so busy, and it was a crazy time, and I kept wanting to tell you. And then the longer I didn't, the more difficult it became. I thought that if you knew that Max was my ex-boyfriend and actually worked at the hotel, you might not want to go any longer. You might think it was too awkward."

"I'm someone who keeps my word, Beth." Frowning, Ava closed her eyes and rubbed at her forehead with the back of her hand. "It was more awkward meeting him and realizing who he was. You should have told me from the beginning – or even sent me a message when I got here! It would have been for the best."

"I wanted to." Beth's voice dropped into a low whisper. "I *did* want to, but it was all so painful. Even thinking about him was difficult."

"I get it, Beth. Really, I do." Biting her lip, Ava's guilt began to burn hotter. Maybe that had been a good reason for her friend not to have told her.

"I just couldn't bear it." Ava winced, hearing the sob catch Beth's voice. "I'm sorry, Ava."

Perhaps I was a little bit too harsh.

"Everything we talked about, every time we mentioned Spring Forest, my heart did this little sickening lurch. I was supposed to be excited about going there, and then I would remember everything Max and what he did, and my heart would just tear apart all over again." It sounded like Beth was swallowing her sobs, and Ava immediately began to reassure her.

"Listen, don't worry. I get why you didn't want to bring it up. I guess I should have been more understanding."

Beth hiccuped. "Really?"

"Of *course* you didn't want to talk about him. I can't imagine how you must have felt or how difficult it was planning a conference here and trying not to think about Max." Taking in a breath, she shrugged. "It just came as a bit of a surprise, that's all."

"Thanks, Ava." The sob was gone from Beth's voice. "It's been really hard. I couldn't bear the thought of seeing him. Every time we talked about the conference and even what meals the authors would have, I would just hear his voice in the back of my mind, telling me that his life would be better off without me."

I'd forgotten about that. Max was really harsh with her.

Shaking her head to herself, Ava tried to reassure her friend. "You don't need to worry about me, Beth. I'm not about to give him even a minute of my time."

A quiet, broken laugh followed. "He's got everyone in that town wrapped around his little finger. He's a volunteer firefighter, so a lot of them think he's this great guy who does no wrong. They ignore all of his faults and flaws, just smile at him and think how amazing he is. No doubt everyone in Spring Forest will think that *I'm* the problem, not Max."

"Not me," Ava replied firmly. "I don't know Max, but I know what he did, so he can't take advantage of me to try and get me on his good side. Don't worry, Beth. I'm not about to let him charm me in the same way he's charmed everyone else."

"Thanks, Ava."

At least Beth's not crying anymore. Sorry that she had been the one to upset her friend in the first place, Ava took a breath and changed the subject. "Got any plans this evening?"

Beth laughed. "I do, actually." Her smile was back, and Ava let out a slow breath of relief. "I'm going out with a friend. An old friend that I haven't seen in ages." There was happiness in her voice that made Ava smile. "I'm really looking forward to it."

"I'm glad."

"What about you?"

"What *about* me?" Ava laughed, shaking her head. "All I'm planning is an early night. This conference is tiring me out!"

A horrified, mock gasp came through. "That's the last thing you should do. Spring Forest is a great little town, and you're not there for long – unless you decide to take up the offer head office is sending your way – so you should definitely go explore. Spring Forest is gorgeous at Christmas time."

Ava blinked rapidly, her smile freezing. "Offer? What offer?"

Her only answer was a breath of silence, and Ava's stomach began to churn, wondering what exactly it was the guys at the top were planning… and how she was meant to be a part of it.

"Yeah, I probably shouldn't have said that."

"But you did." Gnawing the edge of one fingernail, Ava waited for Beth to answer.

Another sigh came. "Okay, so you didn't hear it from me, but the company's thinking about branching out permanently in Spring Forest. *All* the feedback from the conference so far has been amazing. Even though they've only been with you for a couple of days, the authors keep talking about how incredibly inspiring Spring Forest is, and Golden Book Publishing wants to jump on that. They're talking about setting up an author's retreat for the authors we represent, and Spring Forest can hold regular conferences instead of just once a year. If all that happens – and I think it will – then they're going to need someone there full-time. I'm guessing they might come to you first."

"Oh." Mentally, Ava shrugged, relieved that it wasn't as big a deal as she'd thought. If the company asked her, she could just say no. "I can't even start thinking about it right now, not when I've got this conference to get through." Sighing, she sat down on the edge of the bed. "You're right, though. Maybe I should go explore this town for a little while."

"You can't just sit in your hotel room every night. You'll get lonely." Beth laughed, and Ava grinned.

"I'm not about to start falling for some gorgeous small-town boy if that's what you're worried about."

Beth giggled. "Why not? I did."

In that second, Max sprang back into Ava's mind, and her smile quickly faded. *Why do I think about him?*

"Ava?"

Giving herself a small shake, Ava took in a long breath. "I was just thinking about where to go. I have a couple of hours to kill, so tell me some good places to go."

"Great!" Beth's encouragement made Ava smile, forgetting all about Max. "First, I'd just go wander down the town's Main Street. They'll have all those Christmas lights up, and from last year, I remember that Spring Forest does a pretty good job with them. It makes the town look really festive, really heartwarming, you know?"

"Sounds good. I'll definitely do that."

"And then, if you're looking for a quiet drink in a cozy atmosphere, there are two places I'd recommend. One is Rivers Bar and Grill… it's down by the river." She laughed, and Ava shook her head.

I love this town already.

"There's plenty of signs for it, so you should be able to find your way easily."

"And if I can't?"

"If you can't, then there's another place on the main street called Dave's."

Ava's eyebrow lifted high. "Dave's?" she repeated as Beth laughed. "Are you being serious right now?"

"I sure am! And yes, before you ask, the owner's name is Dave. He's great."

Ava shook her head. "Sounds like I'm going to have to go check out that place with a name like that!"

"Send me a picture of you there to prove it."

Grinning at the challenge, Ava found herself suddenly enthusiastic about heading out into Spring Forest. "I sure will. I better get going. I'll call you soon, Beth."

"No problem. And again, I'm sorry about not telling you about Max. I realize now that I should have."

"I understand why you didn't. Bye."

Still smiling to herself, Ava got off the bed and went straight for the bathroom. She was going to have to change into something less business-like if she was going to go out for a drink in Spring Forest. Her mouth twisted as she looked at her reflection. Okay, she had a couple of shadows under her eyes, but those could easily be hidden. Grabbing her makeup bag, Ava smiled to herself as she applied her foundation. After everything she'd worked through these last couple of days, especially with Max, this was going to be exactly what she needed.

***

"Amazing." Breathing out that word, Ava smiled as her breath frosted the air. Beth was right, Spring Forest was beautifully decorated for Christmas. There were tiny twinkling fairy lights going from one side of the street to the other, just over her head, and they were also looped across the windows of every building. There were tiny little Christmas trees along the sidewalk, each glistening with its own set of lights. Every shop or coffee place she'd passed had an amazing Christmas display in its window, some complete with a waving Santa Claus or snowman. There was a lingering scent of gingerbread in the air, probably coming from one of the three coffee places she'd passed so far. All it needed now was just a little snow – although it was cold enough for everything to have a gentle dab of frost.

The whole thing made Ava smile, helping her to forget about the conference, her responsibilities, about Max… this was just what she'd needed to help her relax.

Her eyes caught a small, hanging sign that jutted out from a building straight ahead of her. Frowning, she began to walk toward it, wondering why it stuck out. She quickly realized it didn't have a single Christmas decoration apart from a single string of fairy lights. It didn't exactly scream Christmas.

Her head tipped back, her eyes widening as she read the sign. Laughing, Ava grabbed her phone and quickly took a selfie, making sure to get the name "Dave's" in the photo. With her head down, she quickly sent it to Beth and pushed her way inside.

The sound of faint music had her lifting her head as she walked into the bar. It was bigger than she'd expected, and there were plenty of people around. The tables were all different shapes and sizes, the chairs and stools too, but that didn't seem to matter to anyone. There wasn't a single Christmas decoration in sight, but all the same, it still had a welcoming atmosphere. Ava smiled as she wandered a little farther inside.

I'll order a drink, sit down for a while, and then head back to the hotel.

Still smiling, she headed toward the bar to order a drink, only for a familiar face to catch her eye.

It   was   Max.

Chapter Six

*A*re *you serious right now?*

The minute Ava walked into the bar, Max groaned out loud. Instead of making his way back home as he'd planned, he found himself heading to Dave's, wanting a place to have a drink and forget about everything else for a while.

Except right now, that "everything else" he was trying to forget about was standing at the other side of the bar.

Rolling his eyes, Max muttered something under his breath, picked up his beer, and took a sip, swiveling around on his stool a little so that he wouldn't have to look at her. If she wanted to come here for a drink, then there wasn't much he could do about that, but he didn't need to go over and try to make her feel welcome, not after the way their last conversation had ended.

If she needs someone to talk to, then she can come over here.

"Everything all right?" Dave, the bartender, shot Max a slightly questioning look, but Max just shrugged, watching as Dave set a glass of white wine in front of Ava. He wasn't planning on telling Dave that he was getting himself twisted in knots over her, especially when he didn't know for sure what was going on.

Whenever I least expect it, there she is. Sighing to himself, Max took another swig and set the bottle down on the counter a little harder than he'd meant to.

Dave looked over.

"Uh… another beer, please. Thanks, Dave."

Dave grinned. "Coming right up."

Max grinned wryly and shook his head. No doubt about it –
misery made for good business.

"Shout if you want another."

"Thanks." Max grimaced. "I'll drink this and then get on home.
Add it to my tab?"

Dave nodded. "Sure."

Running his finger around the top of the beer bottle, Max resisted
the urge to follow Ava with his eyes as she walked past him to a
table.

"Where's that dog of yours? I don't think you've had him in here
for a while."

A little relieved that Dave had taken his mind off Ava, Max
laughed. "My neighbor, Mrs. Grey? She's got him tonight. Told me
she's taken him out twice today and he's all tuckered out."

Dave grinned. "Sounds like he's getting spoiled."

"For putting up with me, he deserves it!" Chuckling, Max picked
up his beer as Dave went off to serve someone else. *He's not the
only one who could do with spoiling.*

Rolling his eyes at himself, Max's shoulders slumped, his smile
fading. The last thing he needed to do right now was feel sorry for
himself. Sure, he'd felt rough ever since his breakup with Beth, but
that didn't mean he had to let it overwhelm him. *Something good
will happen soon enough*, he told himself, his mouth tugging to one
side in a small scowl. *It's just taking a while to get here.*

"Don't think I've seen her in here before." Throwing a glance to
his left, Max's scowl darkened at the two guys talking and looking
over their shoulders. His gut told him they were talking about Ava.

"She sure is pretty." The second man chuckled, elbowing the first. "Maybe she's looking for company. Looks like she's here alone, right?"

Max opened his mouth, about to tell them to leave Ava alone, only to remind himself that he couldn't know for sure whether Ava was looking to meet someone. A jealous heat rolled around his core, and he swung his head back toward the bar, looking down at the beer.

"Think I might go over. See if she'd like to talk."

That jealousy was back, blazing like a furnace. Gritting his teeth at the thought of Ava leaving the bar with one of these guys, Max kept his head down, his jaw tight.

"If you don't, then I will."

As the first man got up, Max threw him a look. He was tall and wiry with a shock of fair hair bouncing across his forehead and a confident grin already plastered across his face.

Max hated the sight of it.

Silently reminding himself that the only thing he was planning to do was finish his beer and get on home, Max couldn't help but swivel around on his stool, letting his shoulders hunch forward a little, his hands clasping the beer. He kept his eyes forward, trying not to make it too obvious that he was watching Ava.

The guy was standing beside Ava's table, saying something to her. Ava was busy looking at her cell phone and only glanced up at him for a second or two.

Doesn't look like she's interested.

Something about that made him smile. It was like he wanted this guy to fail.

The guy gestured to the chair opposite, but Ava shook her head. Max's breath caught as the man grabbed it, pulled it a little closer, and then sat down right next to Ava.

Max scowled, his haunches lifting and his hands clasping a little tighter around his beer. He had no right to do anything, no right to insert himself into the situation, but there was something about the guy that he didn't like... and his instincts were usually right.

Except when it came to Beth.

The first thing that he noticed was that Ava wasn't smiling. She'd set her phone on the table and, it looked like to Max, was narrowing her eyes at the guy in the chair. As Max watched, the man tried to put his arm around her shoulders, but she twisted sharply so that she faced him and then moved back.

Red began to creep into the edges of Max's vision.

Max reached out his hand to grab the guy next to him.

"What's the name of your buddy over there?"

The man next to Max shrugged and jerked his arm away. Max turned toward him a little more, leaning forward on his stool. "I said, what's the name of your buddy?"

"What's it to you?" The man shot a dark glance at Max, clear defensiveness in his eyes.

"I'll tell you what it is to me – that woman over there? I know her. She's one of my friends. You'd better tell me your friend's name so I can go over and get him away from her *quietly* without causing too much of a scene."

The guy snorted. "I don't think you're going to have to take him away from her, it looks to me like he's getting on great."

Max's temper grew. "Listen, I'm going to give you one last chance. Otherwise, it won't just be one guy getting hauled outta here."

The man blinked at Max's aggressive tone, then turned his head toward Dave. "You gonna let him talk to me like that?"

Dave nodded, jerking his chin toward Ava. "If your friend's harassing someone here and you're doing nothing about it, then Max has every right to try and sort it out. If he didn't, I'd do it myself."

"Chad's doing nothing wrong."

Max snorted, shaking his head, his brows heavy over his eyes. "Except it looks to me like *Chad* isn't exactly taking the hint. Looks to me like he's planning on getting what he wants, any way he wants. Excuse me."

Getting off the stool, Max headed straight toward Ava's table, catching her eye as he walked. The man at her table was still talking, still trying to shift closer, and Max's anger began to bottle in his chest. It took all of his inner strength not to grab Chad right out of his chair and shove him toward the door of the bar. Guys like Chad just forced themselves on whatever women they decided they wanted.

"Hi, Ava."

Ava swallowed, struggling to smile. "Hi, Max."

"I saw you come in the bar." Keeping his gaze on Ava just to keep his temper under control, he spread his hands. "I should have come over sooner. Would have saved you the trouble of having to get rid of this guy." Jerking his head in Chad's direction, he finally let his gaze shift over. The man's jaw was working, his eyes flashing, but

Max merely tipped his head toward the door. "Haven't you gotten the picture yet?"

Chad got up quickly, pushing his chair back sharply as it scraped across the floor, coming to stand in front of Max, tipping his chin up.

Max folded his arms across his chest, painting a calm expression on his face even though every single muscle was jumping. "You really need to work harder on your people skills."

"My people skills are just fine." Chad's lip curled, but Max just snorted.

"Even I could tell that Ava doesn't want you here. Let me be clear: If you don't get up and leave Ava alone, then I'll do it for you."

Chad laughed scornfully, his eyes narrowing. "Is that so?"

Gazing back at Chad with a steely gaze, Max nodded slowly as he took one small step closer. "Yeah," he murmured quietly. "Yeah, it is."

For a few seconds, Chad held Max's gaze, then, with a snort, walked straight past Max, slamming his shoulder into his as he went. It took all of his grit not to turn around and go after the guy, clenching his hands into fists as he closed his eyes and sucked air through his nose, waiting for the swell of anger to pass. When he opened his eyes again, Ava had gotten up out of her chair and was coming over to him. Her expression was set, her eyes dancing around the room instead of landing on his face as she pressed her lips together so hard that they were white. Max noticed that there wasn't any color in her cheeks.

"You didn't have to do that."

"I know I didn't. But I wanted to."

Ava bit her lip and then finally looked at him. "Thank you."

"No problem."

She lifted one shoulder, her gaze drifting away again. "He was just a bit… pushy, that's all."

"Don't let Chad give you the wrong impression. Not every man in this town is like him."

"How do you know his name? Are you friends with him?"

Max frowned. What sort of impression had she really gotten of him if she thought he would be friends with someone like Chad?

"I've never met that guy in my life," he told her truthfully. "But when it comes to treating people the wrong way, you'll find me right in the middle of it. What he was trying to do was not okay. But Chad is the exception, not the rule, when it comes to Spring Forest."

"I'll agree with that." Turning slightly, Max saw Dave set another glass of wine on the table by Ava. "On the house. I'm sorry that happened to you. As Max said, the men in this town are nothing like that guy – but if anyone steps out of line, then we've always got guys like Max to stand up and make sure they can't. He's a good guy, this one."

Ava opened her mouth and then, the next second, snapped it closed, shaking her head as she turned it to the side.

What was that for? Had she been about to say something? His gut twisted. *Maybe she's surprised to hear that I'm not all bad.*

"I'd better go." Max waited for half a second, wondering if Ava might ask him to stay and sit with her for a while. But when she nodded and only sent him a quick smile, his heart slammed itself back into place.

That was a dumb thought.

Letting out a long breath, he turned around to head back toward the bar, only for her voice to catch him.

"Max."

He swung back toward her quickly, a slight smile lifting the edges of his mouth, but only silence followed as she bit her lip, turning to go sit back down.

What does she want to say? It was dumb, but Max kept imagining what it would be like to be friends with Ava, to be *closer* to Ava. What was she really like? Would she make him laugh? Or was this serious expression something that she usually wore?

"Ava? What is it?"

Picking up her wine glass, she lifted it toward him in a half toast. "I just wanted to say thank you. I really do appreciate you getting rid of him for me." There wasn't any sort of smile in her voice, and there was a groove forming between her eyebrows as she looked away again. Max swallowed, feeling like a huge chasm had opened between them. The cold in her voice made his heart drop through the floor. He didn't know how to reach her and wasn't sure if she wanted to reach him.

"No problem." Turning, he headed back toward the bar and grabbed his beer, shifting it from hand to hand as it spun across the counter. His head ached. What was going on with him? He had to find a way to push Ava out of his head, and it shouldn't matter to him whether she was friendly to him. After all, she was only going to be here until just before Christmas. Why should he care about anything she did or said? It just didn't make sense.

Max drained the rest of his beer, set the bottle down, and muttered a goodbye to Dave. Sticking his hands in his pockets, he headed to the door. All the while, the urge to turn his head to look over at Ava began to burn up through him. Frustrated, he yanked the door open, hard. Misjudging it, the door hit the edge of his foot just as he was about to step forward, and he cracked his head on the edge. The sound seemed to carry through the room, and right away, the ache in his head billowed, making his vision blur.

"Max? You okay?"

Max couldn't even bring himself to look back over his shoulder, sure that Ava had seen exactly what he'd done. Waving one hand in Dave's direction, he headed out into the night, hoping that the cold air would cool his red-hot face.

The Christmas lights did nothing to lift his spirits. The waving Santa with his jolly grin just seemed to mock Max even more, and he dropped his head forward, shielding his view.

"Max?" Lifting his head sharply, Max took a step back in surprise when Brandon and Heather grinned back at him, the Christmas lights sending sparkles of light over their faces.

"What are you guys doing here?"

Heather smiled at him. "Thought we'd go to Dave's for a drink. You're welcome to join us."

The thought was a kick to his stomach. "I've just come from there, actually. Think I'm gonna head on home."

"Really?" Brandon frowned. "Not like it's really late or anything."

Max shrugged. "Thanks, but I'm sure. Don't want to be the third wheel!" It was a bit of a poor excuse, but from the way that Heather laughed, it looked like she, at least, believed him.

"Your loss." Shrugging, Brandon wrapped one arm around Heather's shoulders. "We'll enjoy the evening without you well enough."

Max grinned as Heather elbowed Brandon in the side.

"Oh, and remember, we've got that stand-in sous chef starting tomorrow. He's only covering until we can find someone new, but I think he might apply for the job himself. You never know, it might be the easiest hire you've ever made!"

Max nodded, grateful for the reminder. "Yeah, of course, thanks, Heather. All the more reason for me to head home, I guess! Make sure I get enough rest."

Brandon grinned. "Got your alarm set?"

At this, Max let out a bark of laughter. "Before you ask, yes, your alarms worked, and, yes, I am going to be keeping them on even though they drive me crazy."

Laughing, Brandon hugged Heather closer, keeping out the cold. "Okay, well, I guess I'll see you tomorrow."

With a wave, Max stepped away, glad that he had been able to keep the truth about his confusing feelings about Ava to himself. Brandon would just tease him if he knew, and that wasn't what he needed right now.

Except I don't even know what I need right now.

Shoving his hands even deeper into his pockets, Max stalked back along the road toward his truck. He'd gone to the bar to try and get Ava out of his head, and then she'd turned up there. It was like fate was teasing him, making things even more difficult than they already were. He was already trying to get over everything that Beth had left him with and didn't need to get distracted by some pretty face that was only going to be here for a few more days.

Plus, she doesn't even like me.

Hating the kick that came into his heart, Max dug around his pocket for the truck keys. Everything about this was so frustrating. He didn't *want* to keep noticing her, but the fact that she was absolutely stunning didn't seem to help. His eyes seemed to be drawn to her no matter where she was.

"Then I just need to stop looking at her." Rolling his eyes, Max got in the truck and shoved the key in the ignition. It all sounded so simple, as though telling himself that he could forget about Ava was going to make it easy to ignore the fact that she was around. There were so many questions about how she was treating him that he still had to answer. Why had she reacted so badly when she'd heard his name? Why did she have that coldness? Max hadn't done anything apart from that first time, and even then, he'd apologized for it, and she had seemed to accept it. So what had changed?

"And why do I care?" Muttering those words aloud, Max slammed one hand down repeatedly on the steering wheel before dropping his head forward. Maybe his heart was just looking for a distraction, someone to think about instead of Beth and the sheer amount of pain she'd left him in. Other than that, he didn't have an answer as to why Ava Patterson was still happily sitting right in the middle of his head, refusing to budge, refusing to leave, and completely refusing to let him forget her.

Chapter Seven

Ava flicked her hair in the mirror, pressing her lips together hard, making sure that her lipstick was perfect. She smiled to herself, one hand on her hip as she tipped her head… and then closed her eyes with embarrassment, her hand dropping back to her side.

What am I doing? It's not like I've got anyone here I need to dress up for. I'm here as a business representative, remember?

Sighing, she shoved all of her stuff back in her makeup bag, trying not to remind herself of the fact that it had been a while since she'd had a date. Yes, there were a few guys in her past – but the two she'd been serious with hadn't been right for her. The first one wanted to travel, while Ava wanted to stay put. The second hadn't wanted to think about the future, and that had been a deal breaker for her.

And since then?

Shaking her head, Ava walked out of the bathroom to find her shoes. Since those dates, work had taken over. Business was going well, but the truth was, she hadn't really given any time to dating, not after the last guy had broken her heart.

Time to think positive.

Day three of the conference had gone well, and Ava finally felt she was settling into the role, getting to know the authors and all their little quirks. The guests were happy, she was happy – everything seemed to be going great… apart from the fact that she hadn't managed to push Max out of her thoughts.

Scowling to herself, Ava looked around for her cell phone as it rang, glancing at the clock on the wall as she searched. *Okay. I've got fifteen minutes. Plenty of time.*

Finally finding her cell in the bathroom, Ava answered it quickly, seeing Beth's name on the screen. There was a lot to tell her, and Beth would want to know how things had gone today.

"Beth, hi. Sorry I didn't call earlier, I've only just gotten back up from the last session, and now I'm getting ready to get back down there. I'm starving!"

"No problem. I wanted to call you to let you know about the amazing feedback we've been getting about the conference! It's all over social media, and everyone here is really happy with how you're doing. I think you should be very proud of yourself, Ava."

Letting out a slow breath, Ava closed her eyes for a second, trying to accept the compliment. "I wasn't always sure that I was going to be able to do this, but I'm so grateful that *you* had confidence in me. This has been a big deal for me, and I'm glad that I haven't let you or the company down."

Beth let out an exclamation. "Let anyone down? You shouldn't even be worrying about something like that, Ava! You're killing it – and the company is moving forward with the Spring Forest office." She took a breath. "How did the book reading go this afternoon?"

Ava laughed, remembering how she'd been so taken with the reading that it had been a struggle to step into her role again. "It went really well. I found it so interesting, and the guests couldn't take their eyes off Lance! I'm not really a fan of science fiction, but by the time he finished reading his chapter, I was already looking up 'Lance Vinson' and thinking about buying the whole series!"

"Sounds great! I wouldn't tell him that you don't read science fiction, but I would *definitely* let him know how much you enjoyed his work. We like to keep our authors happy, remember?"

"I already did." A little smugly, Ava gave herself a little shake, getting her mind back on the plans for the evening. "And everything's organized for tonight." Tonight was going to be the book club conference's Christmas dinner – complete with music, a five-course meal, and a couple of extra Christmas surprises thrown in. Ava's stomach rumbled at the thought of the amazing menu that was headed her way.

"The Christmas dinner was always one of my favorite nights – apart from the last night, of course, when we go all out in that big Christmas party." There was a breath of silence. "I think I'm going to really miss it."

"This is my first one," Ava answered, trying to pull Beth away from that wistful tone beginning to take over her voice. "It all sounds amazing – *and* I hired a guy from town to come and dress up as Santa Claus. I set up a little photo booth in the corner of the room. I thought it would be funny for some of our guests to take their picture with Santa Claus between courses – maybe get a few of them sitting on his knee and stuff like that. If they post to social media, then that will *really* get this conference seen!"

"Sounds amazing. Remember to get them to use the 'Golden Book Publishing' and 'book club conference' hashtags as well, okay?"

Ava smiled. "I sure will."

"Are you all dressed up?"

Looking down at herself, Ava shrugged. "Uh… maybe a little."

"What do you mean, a little?" Beth's voice came screaming down the phone. "*Please* don't tell me that you've just picked out some slacks and a flowery top! I know that's your go-to, but I *also* know that you packed some gorgeous dresses. Why don't you wear one of those?"

Twisting her lips to one side for a few seconds, Emma considered. "I guess I just wasn't sure what someone like me should wear. I'm the host. I'm representing the company."

"But that doesn't mean you can't dress up!" Beth protested. "You go and get changed this minute. Put on something absolutely stunning and go wow our guests. Show them that Golden Book Publishing knows how to enjoy a great time."

A little embarrassed that her friend already knew exactly what she had chosen to wear, Ava walked to the closet, letting out a big, heavy sigh that made Beth laugh. "I really don't want to do this. I think what I'm wearing is just fine."

"Trust me." Beth's voice was firm, refusing to shift even a little. "The guests are going to love seeing you having as much fun as they are. And I want a picture with you and Santa, okay?"

Ava opened her mouth to protest, thought better of it, and shrugged. "Sure, okay."

"You have to be sitting on his knee," Beth continued before Ava could find anything to say. "It'll be amazing for the company's promotional materials, and I guarantee the social media crowd will go wild for it."

There was no point in complaining. What Beth wanted, Beth got… most of the time, and if Ava was honest, the idea was a good one. A sudden flurry of nerves rolled around in her stomach, but she just closed her eyes and took in a breath, telling herself that she was being ridiculous.

It's just one photo sitting with an old guy dressed as Santa. It'll take two minutes, and then it'll be over, and the guests will see that I'm enjoying the night as much as they are. That's the important thing.

"I'd better go." Taking a deep breath, she tried to smile as she spoke. "I hope you're doing okay yourself, Beth."

"I'm doing a whole lot better now that you're in the Spring Forest, and I'm not," came the reply. "Call me tomorrow, okay?"

Promising that she would, Ava ended the call and then reluctantly looked at the dresses in the closet. Beth had said to wear something that would look great, but she didn't have a ton of options. It was either going to be the little black dress or a much more formal thing with cap sleeves and a long, floor-length skirt. Frowning, Ava shifted through the rest of her clothes.

I was sure I had brought something else. Sighing, she shook her head and pulled out the little black dress. *If I'm going to wear this tonight, then I'll have to pick up something else to wear to the Christmas party on the last night.*

"Okay, Beth." Holding up the dress against herself, she tilted her head as she looked at her reflection in the mirror. "I guess this is going to have to do." Her lip curved. *Going to impress the guests and that Santa Claus,* she thought, laughing softly. *I just hope I can get the photo Beth wants.*

"This is an amazing dinner. Incredible so far!"

Ava smiled as Taylor Ingram, one of the authors, came over to her, glass in hand. "I think so too." They were between courses, having already had two, and with three more to go, some of the guests were moving around the room, talking to each other, laughing, and smiling. There was a comfortable, cozy atmosphere, and now that her stomach wasn't grumbling, Ava was enjoying every moment.

"I'm really enjoying myself," Taylor continued, sounding faintly surprised. "I think this conference should be thrown more often. You'd have so much success with it and authors like us. We absolutely adore it."

Ava lifted her eyebrows. "Really? I would have thought that spending several days with your fans could be quite tricky."

"It can be," Taylor agreed with a smile. "But this time, there's been no problems whatsoever. I don't know whether it's because it's Christmas or the fact that we're in this gorgeous little village… or maybe it's that we've got a great bunch of guests this year, but everything has gone so well. I've enjoyed every minute of it so far, and I'm looking forward to the rest of my time here."

Ava put one hand to her heart. "I'm so glad to hear that." Remembering what Beth had said about the company setting up a permanent base in Spring Forest, she managed another smile. "And I'll pass on your comments to my boss. It would be good for them to know."

Taylor laughed and pressed her arm lightly. "There's no need. I've already emailed them myself. I figured that I should do it myself because there's no way you'd be as complimentary about yourself as I would be, right?" She smiled. "You're different from the one from last year. Not a bit of arrogance about you, is there?"

Something tightened in Ava's throat as she tried to force a smile, suddenly struggling to know what to say. Taylor couldn't be talking about Beth, could she? Inwardly, Ava silently thought that Taylor must be getting Beth mixed up with someone else. "This is my first time running any sort of conference, and the fact that you think I'm doing a good job... " A little surprised at the tightness in her throat, Ava waved one hand. "Let's just say I appreciate it."

"You should have a lot more confidence in yourself. Don't you think you've done a good job?"

Still trying to work out why she was acting so strongly to Taylor's marks, Ava threw out one hand. "I guess. I wasn't the first choice to run it, so I wasn't sure how it would all go. I'm glad to know you're happy with it so far, though!"

"Well, by the time this conference is done, I'm sure you're going to be the first choice from now on, Ava – and I'll be letting the company know that too." With another smile, Taylor stepped away, leaving Ava with such a huge smile on her face, she was confident it wouldn't go anywhere for the rest of the night. *That was probably the nicest thing anyone has ever said to me about my work.*

Still smiling, Ava wandered around the room, wanting to make sure that every guest looked to be enjoying themselves, wanting them to know she was present and here to help if they needed it, while thinking about what Taylor had said. Yes, she did love her job, but perhaps there hadn't been much of a challenge these last few years. Perhaps she had just settled into what she was good at doing without thinking about what *else* she could do. She had never been asked to do a conference before, but then again, she'd never put herself forward for it.

It's not like I don't help with planning. Beth needs me to organize things for the conference every year. If the company wants to have a book club conference more regularly, then maybe I should put myself forward a bit more.

Chewing on her lip, Ava came to a sudden stop, her thoughts thrown from her mind as she watched Santa Claus walk into the room. He was a little taller than she'd expected, and she was surprised when he jumped up and down on the spot, waving at all of the guests.

He must be really fit for a guy his age.

Tilting her head, she let a frown cross her forehead. There was something about him, maybe something in the way he walked, that suggested to her that he was younger than he'd said. Plus, that beard didn't look real – and Peter had said he had a big, thick, white beard. When she'd called, he'd told her how proud of it he was, said it made him a whole lot more authentic as a Santa.

A lot of the guests had gone quiet, watching Santa as he called hello to them all, and, remembering her role, Ava rushed forward, one hand gesturing to him.

"Ladies and gentlemen, Santa Claus has come all the way from the North Pole to visit us this evening!" A ripple of laughter ran around the room as Ava put one hand on Santa's back. "He'll be right over here, beside this photo booth." Stepping to one side, she gestured to the corner where a huge sign emblazoned the words, 'Golden Book Publishing's book club conference' in red and green letters. In front of it was a chair for Santa – more like a throne, with its wooden frame and red velvet cushions – and besides that, a whole lot of props on a table that people could use for their photos.

"Come and get your photo with Santa – and don't forget to use our hashtags when you post on social media!" *Anything for good publicity.*

"Ho, ho, ho!" Santa leaned closer to Ava, his arm going about her waist as she put her hand on his back again. "Come on over, folks! Come and tell me if you've been naughty or nice this year. Either way, I promise you'll get something from my sack!"

At this, almost everyone in the room giggled, and heat tore into Ava's cheeks as she tried to join in. His hand on her waist spoke of strength, and even his voice sounded different from the guy she'd talked to on the phone. Turning her head, she narrowed her eyes as his hand fell from her waist.

Okay, so that's definitely not a genuine beard. Just who is this?

"I do hope you'll come and sit on my knee."

Ava's face grew hotter still as the man playing Santa murmured that in her direction, sending another grin with it. Telling herself he was just playing the part, she smiled but kept her tone businesslike. "I have to take a picture for the business, so yes, I will have to do that at some point."

She tried to laugh lightly, but the sound got stuck in her throat. Santa laughed lightly, turned, and then headed to the photo booth in the corner of the room. For whatever reason, Ava let out a long breath of relief, surprised at how nervous she suddenly was.

Someone obviously stepped in for him. That's no big deal. So long as I've got a Santa here, that's all that matters.

Lifting her chin, Ava nodded, seeing the servers beginning to bring in the third course.

Beth wants a photo for the business, and I may as well just get it over and done with while the guests are too busy eating to look at me. That way, it won't be hanging over my head for the rest of the evening.

"Thought you'd be first in line, huh?"

At the sound of his voice, Ava's face burned all over again. What was it about this guy that was making her react like that? "Uh, sure. As I said, I need one for the company's social media, so… " Turning, she held out her cell phone to the small group of guests who had come over to watch. "Would one of you mind?"

"Sure, no problem, honey." A woman with a very smiley face took it from her, then shooed her toward Santa Claus. "Go on then."

"Great." Taking in a deep breath, Ava headed toward Santa Claus, coming to stand beside him. "This look okay?"

"Nope." A quiet screech ripped from her mouth as Santa caught her hand and tugged her forward. "I don't think that's what you told the guests to do," he commented, green eyes glinting as he grinned. "I thought you told them to sit right on my knee. You should lead by example."

Ava cleared her throat, glad that he had let go of her hand, although he was still waiting for her to make a decision. There was definitely something familiar about him, but right now, she just couldn't place it.

And he's right. I hate that he's right.

"Go on," the woman holding her phone called, urging Ava forward. "It's gonna be a great shot!"

The company needs this. Reminding herself of what was expected, as well as the fact that there was a growing number of guests watching her, Ava forced a smile and then went to perch on Santa's knee.

His arm went to her waist, holding her steady and then, much to her surprise, pulling her a little closer so that she sat a bit more firmly.

"That wasn't so difficult, was it?" His voice in her ear forced her eyes to his. The thick white curls of his fake beard obscured most of his face but looking into those sea-green eyes made Ava's breath hitch, her whole body bursting into tingles as she suddenly became very aware of just how tightly his arm was around her waist.

Her blood began to burn.

"Say 'Christmas'!"

Turning her head back quickly, Ava forced a smile that she was sure didn't reach her eyes. The woman laughed and took more than a few, but after a second, Ava looked back into Santa's face.

Suddenly, she knew who it was – and for whatever reason, that made everything burn a little hotter.

"I know it's you, Max." *Why am I breathing so fast?* "I don't understand. How did you –?"

Max's eyebrows lifted. "Wait, you didn't know that I'd be taking Pete's place? He said he'd call you about it – he's come down with some sort of stomach bug, so I told him I'd do it since I'm not on shift tonight." His lips pressed together for a second. "I wouldn't have been so… friendly if I'd known he hadn't called. I thought you were expecting me."

Ava searched his face for a long moment. Was this the same Max that Beth had told her about? The one who only thought of himself?

Who wanted a life of freedom, a life where he could push away responsibility? Right now, it sure didn't seem like it.

"Hey, you gonna let someone else have a turn?" The giggle that came after the question had Ava scrambling off Max's knee as quickly as she could. Going to get her cell phone, she thanked the smiley woman and then began to walk away, only for Max to call her name.

"Hey, Ava."

She looked over her shoulder, hoping that her face wasn't as red as it felt. "Yes?"

Max grinned, his eyes still twinkling behind the white beard. "You look great tonight."

Ava blinked, another flush of awareness creeping over her. Was that all he wanted to say? Watching him greet the next guest, Ava couldn't help but stare at him, suddenly very conscious of her little black dress. Had he been flirting with her? And if he had, why was she smiling? Why was there a warmth flooding through her? Snapping her head back, she lifted her chin and bit her lip hard.

This can't be happening. I can't let myself think about Max that way. I shouldn't even be noticing him! He's Beth's ex-boyfriend, and she's told me all about him.

Even though she told herself not to, Ava couldn't help glancing over her shoulder as she walked back to her table, her heart screaming for one last look at Max in that costume. His eyes caught hers for just a second and then flashed away again, and Ava caught herself smiling all over again... only for her to stop dead, realize what she was feeling, and squeeze her eyes shut tight.

Oh   no.   This   is   really   not   good.

Chapter Eight

*W*ell, that was fun.

Max grinned, tugging off his white and silver beard. Okay, so it hadn't been something that he'd *wanted* to do, but being Santa for a night had been a blast. Plus, all the guests had wanted to take a ton of photos, and since he was in full costume, it had been easier to lose himself in it.

The best part was being with Ava.

His grin faded a little. He thought she'd known he was Santa, clearly, she had not. Having her so close to him had been incredible, but at the same time, it had set a fire in him that, so far, he hadn't been able to douse.

"I take it that Santa had a lot of fun, then?"

Max turned around just as Brandon walked into the break room. "That would be a yes. Gotta admit, though, I'm surprised that the adults are just as excited to get their picture taken with Santa as kids are!"

Brandon chuckled. "I bet it wasn't exactly hard work for you, either."

"I won't pretend that it was all bad." Going to sit down on one of the comfortable chairs, Brandon tipped his head a little to the left. "It's good to see you smile like that. I don't think I've seen you look this way since... well, since Beth."

It was like a cloud had covered the sun. Max shrugged and turned his head away, swallowing his smile.

"I get that you don't want to talk about it a whole lot, but she really hurt you. Whether you want to admit to that or not, I can still see it. And you know that if there's anything I can do then – "

"Thanks, but there isn't." Breaking in through Brandon's conversation, Max shrugged out of his Santa coat, aware that he'd spoken a little more curtly than he'd meant.

"Okay."

The silence that followed made Max scowl. *Brandon's just trying to help, and I've never really let him in.* He hadn't talked to anyone about what had happened, not really. Maybe it was time to try and open up, no matter how awkward he felt doing it.

Max took in a breath.

"Everything just feels a little bit darker since I broke up with her," he admitted, hating how everything inside him twisted up when he spoke about Beth. "I guess I'm just trying to find a way out of that."

Brandon gave him a small nod, his eyes searching Max's face. "It can be difficult to find a way out of that sort of place when you've given so much of yourself to a relationship."

With a wry smile that agreed with everything Brandon said, Max began to unbutton the Santa costume waistcoat at the back. "I appreciate that Brandon. It was just all so sudden, you know?"

Brandon said nothing, holding Max's gaze for a second.

"We were pretty serious about each other… or at least, I thought we were. But then she… "

It hurt. Speaking like this, telling Brandon what had happened – it was like a physical pain that just grew and grew, but it seemed like the right thing to do. The pain was cathartic, needing to be shared so that he could heal, something that would help him move past the shadows that still clung to the edges of his life. "I was going to ask her to marry me, Brandon. I thought she was the one."

Max caught the way his friend's eyes widened a little, but initially, Brandon didn't say anything. The significance of what Max had said seemed to sink into the silence, making the air feel heavier as he dragged it into his lungs.

"I'm sorry, Max."

Max turned away a little, setting the waistcoat on top of the Santa jacket before working on the belt. "Sorry" hadn't been what he expected to hear.

"I'm sorry for everything you're working through right now," Brandon continued quietly. "I never knew that was what you were planning. You guys seemed like such a good fit, so now that I think about it, yeah, I understand it. And then for her to go and do that… "

"Yeah, it was a bit of a shock," Max admitted. "But then I realized that I didn't want to be with someone that I didn't really know – and I definitely didn't know Beth. Clearly, she wasn't as happy as I thought," His shoulders lifted as he managed to tug the belt free, grabbing at the pants with one hand as they threatened to fall down around his ankles. "I should be glad that we ended things before it was too late, but if I'm honest, I'm still broken up about it. I had strong feelings for her."

Brandon sat forward in his chair. "I can't imagine what that must be like. One day you're about to propose, and the next, you break up."

With a small smile, Max fell back into one of the chairs and began to tug off the big, black boots. He couldn't get the pants off without taking the boots off first. "It's rough, is all I can say." *I wish I could share more details. I'm just not ready to talk about it. Why reopen the wound?*

Getting up, Brandon patted Max's shoulder as he walked over to the counter. "Take time to recover, buddy. It's not exactly a small thing that happened."

"No, it's not."

"Coffee? I'm getting decaf."

Max tugged off the other boot. "Sure." Sitting back in his chair, he took the mug of decaf coffee from Brandon, waiting for his friend to sit down. "In terms of what happened with Beth, though, I figure the only thing I can do is accept what happened and try to work through things."

Adding some cream to his coffee, Brandon stirred it slowly, a thoughtful expression on his face as his eyes drifted away from Max. "Yeah, I guess," he muttered, wandering over to join Max at the chair. "It helps, I suppose, if there's someone else who catches your eye at the same time." A small smile lifted his mouth as Max frowned, hoping that defense might help Brandon to drop the subject.

"Don't think that Heather and I didn't see Ava sitting at Dave's." Laughing, he arched one eyebrow. "Was that the reason that you took off in such a hurry?"

Max groaned. "Don't tell me. She told you guys all about what happened."

"Her knight in shining armor," Brandon grinned, although that disappeared quickly. "In all seriousness, though, I'm sure she appreciated that. The other guy sounded like a jerk."

Sipping some of his coffee, Max grimaced, remembering the arrogant smile on the man's face. "Yeah, he sure was. But when it comes to Ava, things are, well, weird."

"Weird?"

"Weird." Not knowing how else to express it, Max's lips twisted. "It's like she can't look at me right now, and then when I go to speak to her, everything gets a bit muddled, and I end up saying things I don't mean to say. It's driving me crazy."

Brandon rolled his eyes. "You sure that's not in your head? The first part, I mean. And when it comes to you, maybe the fact that you like her is making you even more aware of her reaction to you. Or maybe you're confused with everything you're feeling right now."

"I'm not feeling anything," Max retorted swiftly – probably a little too quickly, given the way Brandon grinned. "Anyway, that would be a dumb idea."

"Why would it be dumb? I've only chatted with Ava a few times, but she seems like a nice person."

"First, because she isn't here to stay," Max shot back, not wanting Brandon to begin to sing Ava's praises. "And second, because starting a quick fling with Ava just to get over Beth wouldn't be a good idea."

"I wasn't thinking of a fling," Brandon answered, waving one hand. "That's not your style. I just thought that you'd done long distance once. Is there any reason you couldn't do it again?"

Max opened his mouth and then shut it, his forehead wrinkling. "The truth is, I'm not sure I'm ready for something new. I have to figure out what I'm looking for, what I want." *Okay, so that last part isn't exactly the truth. I already know what I want – someone who will commit, someone who will be honest with me… and who looks amazing in a little black dress.*

That last thought had him rubbing one hand over his eyes, forcing it away.

"Okay." Brandon nodded slowly, dragging the word out. They'd been friends for long enough that Max could see that Brandon didn't believe him. "Or maybe – and I'm not saying I'm right about this – maybe you're just using this as an excuse not to chase after whatever is going on between you and Ava." After finishing his coffee, Brandon got up out of his chair, clapped Max on the shoulder, then jerked his head toward the door. "I'd better get back. My break's just about over. See you tomorrow."

Max lifted his hand. "See you tomorrow. Sorry you got stuck on the late shift."

"I don't mind it too much, it's usually pretty quiet, although I do miss Heather." A smile crossed his face. "She's getting prepped for the Christmas party tomorrow night. You are still coming to that, aren't you?"

"Uh… sure."

Brandon frowned. "Still no plus one?" His eyes twinkled, but Max only rolled his. "I'll take that as a no." Laughing, Brandon headed out the door, leaving Max shaking his head with a cup of lukewarm coffee in his hand. His thoughts were whirling all over the place ever since he'd opened up to Max about Beth, and he wasn't ready to head home. For half a second, Max thought about going to Dave's but shook his head. He couldn't be sure that Ava wasn't going to be there, and after everything he'd felt this evening, seeing her again probably wasn't a good idea.

Tipping his head back, Max rested it against the chair and closed his eyes. He couldn't seem to get Ava out of his thoughts. That little black dress had clung to every inch of her, and even now, the memory of her sitting on his knee sent heat curling up through him, flooding his veins. She had been so close to him, her blonde hair draped over one shoulder, a hint of strawberries around her as her blue eyes had scrutinized him, trying to work out who he was.

I only wish she'd smiled.

"Max?"

He shot up in the chair, his coffee slopping dangerously to one side of the mug as he saw the very person he'd been trying to forget standing in the doorway. How long had she been there?

"Ava, hi." Setting his coffee down, he got up out of his chair – and his red Santa pants immediately flopped down to his ankles, revealing green boxer shorts covered with cartoon polar bears.

Letting out a choking sound, Max scrambled to pull them up, his face burning with humiliation.

I should have left the belt on.

Standing up, he grabbed the side of his pants to keep them up and dared a glance at Ava. One hand covered her mouth, but her eyes were sparkling with laughter, and Max scrubbed his other hand over his face as though he could get rid of his red face that way.

"Sorry about that."

She dropped her hand, the corners of her mouth edging up. "No problem." She was still wearing her Christmas dress, leaning against the door frame, and Max felt like the court jester in front of a queen. Dropping his head, he came a little closer, wishing he hadn't embarrassed himself after what had been an amazing evening.

"Brandon said I could find you here. Aren't you off shift?"

He lifted his head. "Yeah, I am. I just needed to relax for a few minutes before I went home. I hope nothing's wrong?"

Ava smiled at him. There was a brightness in her eyes that he hadn't seen before, genuine warmth, and that smile that just seemed to keep on growing. His embarrassment began to fade.

"Nothing's wrong. The opposite, in fact." She took a breath, then came a little further into the room. "I just wanted to come and say thank you for what you did in stepping in for Santa like that. I'm guessing the last thing you need after a busy day is to dress up as Santa and come to the Christmas party."

Her eyes flickered as she smiled and laughed from her chest. "Listen, this is a small town, and I knew that if Pete couldn't do it, then nobody would be able to step in last minute." Smiling, he tipped his head. "It was no problem. It was a little more fun than I thought it would be."

"I'm glad about that. I'll make sure you get paid for your time."

"I don't care about that." Max gave her a brief smile. "I just wanted to help so that you wouldn't be let down. There were a lot of people putting their pictures on social media from what I could tell, so I hope it has a good impact."

To his surprise, Ava reached out and pressed his arm for a second, her eyes dancing. "You have no idea how much this has blown up on social media." Letting out a quiet laugh, she shook her head. "I think you've become a bit of a hit online in the publishing and book lovers community!" Dropping her hand back to her side, she tipped her head, looking up at him with a soft smile and pulling at her mouth as though she were seeing him with fresh eyes. "Next year, you might get asked to play Santa again!"

He grinned. "Well, if you're the one asking me, Ava, I'll guarantee I'll say yes."

Where did that come from?

Ava's eyes widened a little. For a second, he thought she would mumble something and hurry away, but instead, she took in a long breath as her smile remained steady. "You're very sweet, Max." She spoke quietly as if she was trying to work out exactly what it was about him that she couldn't get her head around. "And you never know, I might take you up on that."

Finding himself delighted with her reaction, Max lifted an eyebrow. "You mean you'll be back here next year?" For whatever reason, the thought of never seeing her again sent his heart into a tailspin.

"Maybe. It depends."

Caught somewhere between disappointment that she would be gone for an entire year and excitement that he wouldn't have to say goodbye for too long, Max set his shoulders as he drew in a breath. His smile faded as he chased away those thoughts. *I've just gotten out of a long-distance relationship, and that didn't exactly end well. Even thinking about starting another one would be foolish.*

"The company I work for is thinking about having a presence here in Spring Forest all year round. The authors at this year's retreat absolutely love it here, so the company is considering having a retreat here for authors, as well as making the book club conference more than just once a year." Her eyes dropped away from his, her mouth pulling into a flat line. "I'm not sure what Golden Book

Publishing wants from me yet, though. They might offer me the position, and they might not. Hard to tell."

Seeing the uncertainty on her face, Max reacted on instinct, catching her fingers for a second. "Why *wouldn't* they offer you the job? From what I've heard, everyone here thinks you're doing great. They love it, and that's got a whole lot to do with you."

Ava blinked, looking back into his face as her fingers slowly began to wrap around his. Electricity shot a bolt straight through his heart, his mouth went dry, and the awareness that they were completely alone in the break room suddenly hit him right between the eyes. He didn't – couldn't – move. There was something here for sure, but part of him was too afraid to find out exactly what it was.

"Maybe." Ava sighed as Max dropped her hand, suddenly overwhelmed by the amount of feeling breaking through him. He hadn't felt like that in a long time – in fact, he was sure he had never felt like this before. That instant connection, that sudden spark, the way his heart tumbled over and over… that hadn't even happened with Beth.

"I should probably head back to my room." As if she knew there was a whole lot going on in Max's head, Ava took a step back. "Thanks again, Max. I really appreciate what you did."

Max blinked, clearing his thoughts as he looked down at her, seeing the sudden flash of doubt in her eyes, the way her mouth tugged down. "If you're worried that it's other people that make this conference great, you're wrong, Ava." The fervency in his voice was strong, ebbing through every word. "I saw you tonight – you're great at what you do. *You're* the one who makes this conference happen. *You're* the one who makes sure every single person is happy. *You're* the one who checks every little detail, making it all run smoothly. Don't think for a second that you're not worthy of all this praise, Ava. You absolutely are."

Somehow, he'd moved closer to her, and when she tilted her chin a little, looking up at him with those blue eyes that reminded him so much of a clear blue sky on a sunny day, the heat that seared through Max was overwhelming. The urge to grab her by the shoulders and kiss her long and hard was tremendous, to the point that Max let out a shuddering breath and stepped back a little. The air grew thick, and he swallowed hard, confused by the intensity that scorched the air between them.

"Thanks, Max. I appreciate that."

She licked her lips, made to say something more, then shook her head before waving one hand and heading out of the break room.

Max stared after her, his chest heaving furiously. For the life of him, he couldn't work out exactly what was going on between him and Ava – they'd gone from coldness to overpowering heat in no time at all, and it wasn't so little a thing anymore.

Running both hands through his hair, Max let a groan run through his lips as his colossal Santa breeches fell down around his ankles again. His eyes closed.

Great. What am I supposed to do now?

Chapter Nine

"Thank you all so much for your questions. I think we'll take three more and then head for lunch."

Hands raised around the room. Ava looked around at all of the guests sitting at long rectangular tables. A lot of them had taken notes, wanting to know exactly how their favorite authors came up with so many brilliant stories. Ava was just happy to listen.

She chose one person – an older gentleman with horn-rimmed glasses, and then settled back in her chair, letting the question flow and the author answer. After a few minutes, it was time to pick the second and, after that, the third and final one.

"My question is for Danielle Phillips."

Ava nodded, gestured to the romance author, and then sat back down. Her stomach grumbled and she flushed with embarrassment, hoping that the authors near her hadn't heard it.

"What I love about your books is the way they express that spark that just happens between the man and the woman." The woman twirled her blonde hair with her finger as she looked down at her notebook. "Some of your books have a lot of characters. I just wondered how you knew which ones would have that spark and which ones wouldn't – do you plan for it, or does it just happen when you write? Sometimes it seems like the most unlikely pair end up together."

A zip of lightning ran down Ava's back, and her mind suddenly flooded with thoughts of Max, her lips curving as she remembered how he'd stood up just as his pants had fallen. A glimpse of those muscular thighs had sent all sorts of thoughts running through her, but in the end, she'd just laughed.

And why am I thinking about that right now?

Sighing quietly, Ava gave herself a small shake. She had no idea where that image had come from or why that question had sparked her thinking about him, but for whatever reason, she couldn't seem to chase him away. Taking in a breath, Ava tried to concentrate on the answer, reminding herself that lunch would be coming soon and she would have to be ready to announce it so that the guests couldn't ask any more questions.

"But isn't that a great thing?" the author began as a murmur of approval ran around the room. "Sometimes that's how things are. We might meet someone and hit it off with them in a way that we never expected, feeling things that we tell ourselves we shouldn't feel."

The words dug into Ava's heart. Wasn't that exactly how she felt?

"I think what's important is to make sure that the main character ends up with someone who, regardless of what they've gone through, has a genuine heart. They might have to prove their love, might have to prove that they've changed, but sometimes that's what life demands of us." The author laughed softly. "Every one of us has bad habits, character flaws. All of us have made mistakes. I don't think there's a single one of us who could say we've never hurt someone else. Maybe we've said a spiteful word, been envious, or judged someone unfairly – but those things don't define who we are. There is a place for forgiveness, for an apology, for healing. Isn't that part of what makes a great story?"

Ava closed her eyes, running her fingers through her hair. She lowered her head, setting her elbows on the table as she let out a long, slow breath. Everything Danielle said made Ava think of Max. It was like she had looked right into Ava's heart, reminding her of the fact that she *had* judged Max from the minute she'd met him, but didn't everyone have bad days, just like Danielle had said?

But what about what Beth told me about him? She wouldn't have said anything that wasn't true.

Her forehead creased as she squeezed her eyes closed for the second time.

"But there are always two sides to every story," the author finished. "I want to make sure that I portray my characters as real, genuine, sometimes difficult people who get mixed up and confused and lost – and show what *their* perspective is on the other characters. Does that make sense?"

It makes too much sense. Grimacing inwardly, Ava took in a deep breath and then lifted her head. Everyone in the room was looking at her. A fire burned in her belly, shooting up flames to her chest and neck. "Sorry, everyone." Picking up her pen, she doodled it nervously on her blank notebook paper. "I'm guessing I'm not the only one entranced by the authors' answers today!"

That brought a lot of smiles, and the tightness in Ava's chest began to uncoil. The door at the end of the room opened, and Ava caught Brandon sticking his head in. He gave her a smile and a thumbs-up, and Ava pushed herself off the table. Returning his thumbs-up, she got out of the chair. "And it looks like lunch is ready. So, if you guys want to make your way to the dining room, we'll be back here in ninety minutes."

Waiting until everyone filed out, Ava followed after them all, trying to knock away all those unsettling thoughts about Max. She was thinking too much about him, losing her focus instead of concentrating on the conference. *I'm going to make a mistake if I let myself become distracted.* Taking in a deep breath, she lifted her chin, pushed open the door, and headed straight for the dining room.

"This looks amazing."

Ava looked down at her plate, nodding as she agreed with Danielle. "I went for the chicken salad, too. Gotta say they make even a pile of green leaves look appetizing!"

Her stomach growled again, and Ava closed her eyes with embarrassment as Danielle laughed, elbowing her gently. "You've been working too hard." Picking up her knife and fork, she hovered over her plate. "Go on. I think you should get to eat first since you're the one who's been working really hard."

Ava laughed and shook her head. "I'm just doing my job."

Danielle shrugged. "All the same. You go first."

Stabbing her fork down into the salad, Ava speared a piece of chicken, snagging some salad with it. Popping it into her mouth, she chewed, swallowed, and closed her eyes. "Wow, it's amazing." Gesturing to Danielle's plate with her fork, she waved it around. "Try some! I'm sure you'll love it."

"Wait!"

Ava's fork clattered onto her plate as Max ran across the room toward their table. His eyes weren't fixed on her, however, but on Danielle. His face was flushed and his chest heaved as he came to a stop right in front of them, eyes flashing with worry. "I'm so sorry. Have you touched this?" Gesturing to her plate, he put both hands at his waist as Danielle shook her head.

87

Seeing this, Max blew out a huge breath, his shoulders dropping as his eyes closed.

"Max." Ava's eyes went from one to the other. "Is something wrong?"

Max barely glanced at her. "We have a stand-in chef in the kitchen at the moment," he explained, reaching out to take Danielle's plate. "I don't think he got the memo about there being an egg allergy. I came in early to make sure that everything was okay for lunch and mentioned it in passing. The look on his face told me that he'd missed that completely. I'm so, so sorry."

Ava blinked. "It's a chicken salad, Max."

A tiny smile touched his mouth, but his gaze kept dropping away from her. "Yes, it is, but there are traces of egg in the dressing. I remember you saying that it was a severe allergy, Ms. Phillips. I can only apologize." Taking a small step back, plate in hand, he dropped his head, his eyes lowering to the floor. "On behalf of the hotel, I want to apologize for this dreadful mistake. It should never have happened, and I can assure you it will never happen again."

Ava glanced at Danielle, taking in her calm expression, although she wasn't smiling. Choosing to stay silent, Ava tied her fingers together under the table, pressing her lips against each other hard as she waited for Danielle to speak.

This could all go really badly.

"Please don't worry."

Reaching across the table, Danielle touched Max's arm for a second as he lifted his head. "Nothing happened. You managed to get to me in time – and since I've just finished telling all of our guests here that everyone makes mistakes, I don't think I can hold it against you!" She smiled. "Thank you for being so vigilant."

Ava let out her tension in a slow, inconspicuous breath as Max swallowed, giving a small shake of his head, unsure what to say.

He's probably as overwhelmed as I am.

"I'm guessing Christmas makes things busy here at the hotel – and you've had to add a stand-in chef into the middle of it all as well!" Danielle continued, her voice gentle. "I understand. I'm not going to sue or anything, but it would be great if I could get another chicken salad. I was looking forward to it, but maybe without the dressing this time, please?"

This edge of laughter in her voice made Ava jerk in surprise. Danielle had almost eaten something that would have thrown her into a severe allergic reaction, and now she was laughing about it. Relief soaked into every part of her, and she finally managed a smile in Max's direction.

"Absolutely. Thank you so much for being so understanding about all of this." He sent a glance to Ava and then looked back at Danielle. "I'm very grateful."

Danielle smiled and shrugged. "It's not your fault – and it's no problem. The food here is delicious, and this salad is going to be no exception, I'm sure."

Max nodded, smiled, and then turned around, heading back toward the door with Danielle's plate in his hand. Danielle was saying something to her, but Ava was too busy concentrating on following Max with her eyes, her heart still beating a little too quickly.

"Ava?"

A gentle hand on her arm made her jump. "Oh, Danielle. I – I'm sorry. Thank you for being so calm about it all."

Danielle laughed. "It's not the first time something like this has happened. It's great he's being so careful, especially when his shift hasn't even started yet."

Murmuring her agreement, Ava absent-mindedly picked up her fork, still thinking about how quickly Max had come rushing into the room.

"He's pretty cute as well." Danielle grinned, and Ava looked over at her in surprise. "I just wanted to see him smile – that frown was doing him no good at all. To be honest, with a smile like that, I'd probably eat anything he put down in front of me!"

A flush came into Ava's cheeks as she tried to stammer something in reply, resisting the urge to rub over her face with one hand.

"And don't think I missed the way he looked at you," Danielle continued. "You're going to have to speak to him."

"Me?" A little surprised, Ava blinked back at Danielle. "Why?"

"Because he'll be worried about the reputation of the hotel," she said quietly. "You need to tell him everything's okay. That must have been stressful for him."

"I'm sure I can do that." Going to speak to Max privately. Again. Emotions passed as she curled one hand into a tight fist. "I'll make sure to do it soon."

***

The final session had gone quickly, and Ava headed to the front desk, expecting to find Brandon there. Smiling at the cute Santa decoration that sat to one side of the reception desk, she rang the bell, and Santa immediately came to life, twirling around on his little ice pond, making her laugh.

And now, whenever I see a Santa, I'm going to remember Max and those enormous red pants.

"Hi, can I help you?"

It wasn't Brandon who emerged from the small side room but someone Ava hadn't seen before. A little off-balance, given that she had expected Brandon, who had already told her once before where Max was, Ava bit her lip, reading the man's name tag. "Uh… hi, James. I'm Ava. I'm running the book club conference here at the hotel. There was an incident today with the food, and I was wondering if I could speak to the head chef he's still here."

A small frown flickered across James' forehead. "I'm sorry to hear that. Would you like to speak to the manager?"

Lifting her hands urgently, Ava quickly shook her head. "No, no, nothing like that. I just wanted to reassure him that everything turned out okay. Would it be possible for me to do that?"

The receptionist hesitated and then, after a second, smiled warmly. "That's very kind of you."

"It's no trouble."

The man picked up the phone and sat just to one side of the desk. "Let me just give him a call. He'll be up here in a second."

Ava caught his arm, then blushed at her forwardness. "Sorry – it's just that I don't want to be a bother. I can easily head to the kitchen to see Max if that would be okay. I'm guessing it's closed for the evening already."

The man hesitated, then smiled. "You know Max?"

Ava looked away. "Only a little. Well enough to know that he'll be busy making sure that everything's ready for tomorrow." *Especially after what happened today.*

James laughed, his eyes kind. "Then you *do* know him. Sure, that's no problem. Let me just call him to let him know you're on your way."

It felt like birds were flapping their wings in her stomach as she made her way through to the kitchen. There was something about Max that always seemed to set her alight, but it never felt like a bad thing. It was almost as though she *wanted* to feel that way which was, of course, incredibly stupid since Max was Beth's ex-boyfriend and had treated her horribly. Scowling to herself, she pushed open the door and stepped inside. Max turned to look at her, his light expression quickly fading as he saw her frown.

"Ava, is something wrong? It's about lunch, isn't it? I thought she seemed far too quick to forgive the mistake. I'm so sorry."

Before she could respond, Max had strode across the kitchen and taken her hands, looking down into her eyes with a furiously fervent gaze. "I swear it was an accident. If this causes any trouble for the company or for the hotel, then –"

"There's nothing wrong." Squeezing his hands firmly, Ava looked up into his face, seeing his eyes round. "I just came to make sure you were okay – and from the look of you, I'm glad I came."

Max stared at her for a long moment, and Ava found herself holding her breath as if she was expecting something. Then, he dropped her hands, threaded his fingers through his hair, and turned around, his shoulders were rounding as he lowered his head. The breath he let out was so obvious that it made Ava smile softly, practically feeling the relief emanating from him. Max was obviously someone who took things seriously, feeling them in the depths of his heart. Had he been worrying about this, thinking that she was going to come by at some point and tell him that Danielle had changed her mind? That she would sue the hotel after all?

"Sorry." Swinging back to her, Max dropped his hands. There was a wry smile on his face. "From the look on your face, I thought you were going to come and tell me something awful."

"Oh." A little frustrated with herself for keeping the scowl on her face when she walked into the kitchens, she glanced away. "Sorry, that look wasn't for you. It was, I mean, I was just thinking about something else."

"Right." Max gestured to the empty kitchen. "If you came here looking for food, I'm afraid everything's cleaned up."

Laughing, Ava shook her head. "No, I just wanted to make sure you were okay. I could tell that what happened affected you – although I think you handled it well. Danielle didn't have a bad word to say about you after you left. Quite the opposite, actually."

Max's smile was gone in a second. "It should never have happened in the first place. If she'd gone into anaphylactic shock, then I don't know what I would have done."

Concerned by the worry in his expression, the lines that formed around his eyes as he frowned, Ava found herself moving forward, not quite sure what she planned to do but wanting to reassure him all the same as her hand reached out to him. "But that didn't happen, did it?" After a second, she pulled it back to her side, not sure exactly what she had planned to do. Take his hand? Put it on his arm? Lift it to his shoulder? *And then slide it around his neck?*

Clearing her throat, she smiled tightly. "This is exactly why I wanted to come and talk to you. I wanted to make sure that you weren't worrying about anything. Everything is fine."

Max's green eyes seemed to flicker with hints of gold as she held his gaze. It was like he was looking for reassurance from her, wanting to know that everything she said was the truth.

For the second time, Ava's feet moved of their own accord, but Max was the one who stepped back this time, and Ava's heart sank to the floor. Annoyed with herself, she turned around, heading back toward the door. *What exactly was I expecting?*

"Well, I guess I better leave you to finish up with whatever you're doing." The cheerfulness in her voice sounded fake even to her, cringing as she pushed the door open. She was embarrassed for expecting something she kept telling herself she didn't want – and definitely couldn't let herself have. "Goodnight."

Max's footsteps were quick behind her. "Ava, wait."

Turning around, she looked back at him, wondering why her heart was still doing that crazy dance in her chest. "Yeah?"

He opened his mouth, his eyes dancing across the room away from her. He closed it again, then stuck one hand in his pocket, perhaps trying to look casual, but the pose screamed awkwardness. "Brandon and Heather are having a Christmas party tonight. I said I'd show up for a little while at least." Shrugging, he dropped his head, still not looking at her. "You would be welcome to come along. If you like, I mean. I don't know if you have plans or –"

"Sure, I'd love to." Her response was immediate and Max's head jerked up, his eyes widening.

"Really?"

The birds were back in her stomach again. "Yeah, why not?" *Too late for me to back out now.* "Not sure I have much to wear, though. I've got one outfit for the conference Christmas party, but that's it."

"What you're wearing is great." The words tumbled out of him in a rush. "It's not going to be like one of your big city parties. Just casual. Fun. That sort of thing. No one will mind what you wear."

Ava found herself smiling. "I've never been one for those big formal parties anyway. This sounds great."

For a second, they both looked at each other, and then Ava laughed, shaking her head. "Okay, I'd better go get organized. Will I meet you at the front desk?"

"Sounds good."

"Great."

Waiting until the door closed, Ava paused for a second, one hand going to the wall as she dropped her head.

What am I doing?

She could no longer pretend that she didn't want this. This attraction to Max wasn't going anywhere, and right now, going with him to a Christmas party was something that made her heart sing.

But what about what Beth told me? Max was so cruel. He broke up with her for no reason and then told her he wanted no part of her. How cold.

Lifting her head, Ava headed back to her room. What Beth had said about Max didn't seem to line up with the person she was getting to know. Maybe something more had happened. Maybe, like Danielle said, there were two sides to every story. So far, Ava had only heard one.

Time for that to change. A sudden excitement sent fireworks through her. *I'm going to a Christmas party with Max. Everyone knows that anything can happen at a Christmas party.*

Chapter Ten

"**I**'m pretty sure you said you weren't going to bring anyone."

Max blinked. "What?" It took him a second too long to drag his eyes away from Ava, a second that Brandon noticed, and his smile got much too big.

"Sorry, am I interrupting something?"

Max cleared his throat and picked up a glass of something – anything – to distract Brandon from who he'd been looking at. "Yeah, this is a great party. Thanks for inviting me. The whole place looks great." Heather had gone all out on decorating the house – but it was classy, not gaudy. The Christmas tree in the corner was magnificent, stretching its tall boughs out toward the roaring fire in the middle of the room, where two stockings hung on either side of the mantlepiece. Christmas songs played in the background, and the cozy atmosphere encouraged conversation and laughter.

Ava seemed to be hitting it off with everyone. What wasn't so great was that she wasn't talking to *him*.

"Max." Laughing out loud, Brandon shook his head. "That was an answer to a question I didn't ask." Shooting Max a pointed look, he grinned. "But thanks. I'm glad you're enjoying the party. I hope Ava is, too."

The way he said Ava's name, emphasizing it, made something begin to curl in the pit of Max's stomach. Something that made him uncomfortable.

"I think she is." Sniffing as though he didn't care, Max turned his head away from Ava. There hadn't been a plan to invite her to the

Christmas party. He hadn't thought about it and wondered what she would say if he did – those words had left his mouth without him even *thinking* about inviting her. And then he'd been so thrilled when she'd said yes, he hadn't been able to stop smiling the whole time she'd gone to get ready.

I'm in dangerous territory.

"Listen, if you like this girl, then there's nothing to be embarrassed about." Leaning in a little bit, Brandon swung one arm around Max's shoulders. "I won't tell anyone."

Max rolled his eyes, snorted, and shoved Brandon's hand away. "Stop it."

Brandon stepped back, something snapping in his eyes, no smile on his face now. "I don't understand why you're trying to pretend you don't have feelings for her."

"Because I *don't*." The sharp response had Brandon's eyes glaring as Max cringed inwardly, embarrassed at how quickly he'd tried to defend himself. Sighing, he closed his eyes. "In case you haven't guessed, Brandon, I'm feeling really uncomfortable about all this."

There was a breath of silence. "You know, I think that's the most honest thing you've said to me about this," he said softly. "Why are you so bothered about how you feel about Ava? Why are you trying to pretend that you don't feel anything – pretend even to yourself?" His friend glanced over at her. "You haven't been able to stop watching her for the last thirty minutes."

Max opened his eyes, seeing the concern that filled Brandon's face. Being open and honest didn't come easily to Max but keeping quiet wasn't going to help him either.

"Because… " A heaviness drew lines across his forehead. "Because after Beth, I didn't think I wanted to start seeing anyone new. She kind of left a hole in me."

"Maybe a hole that someone like Ava can fill," Brandon suggested, no hint of laughter or teasing in his voice. "Now that I know more about what happened with Beth, I feel like I need to remind you that not every woman is like that. No doubt about it, Beth treated you badly, Max. But that doesn't mean Ava will."

Max shook his head, every fiber of his being straining to look over at her again until he couldn't resist any longer. Even though he told her not to worry about what she would wear, she'd changed anyway, wearing the same black dress she'd seen her in a couple of nights ago, although this time, with a cozy white long-sleeve top that fastened with one button at the front. Her long blonde hair trailed gently down her back, and whenever she flipped it over her shoulder, it seemed to ripple like a breeze over the water. His breath seemed to get stolen away as he watched her laugh at something someone had said – and suddenly, all Max wanted to do was walk across the room and stand there with her.

With a grunt, he forced himself to stay where he was, his hand curling tightly. "I've done the long-distance thing before. That was what happened with Beth. I don't think I'm ready to go trying that out again."

Brandon shrugged. "That meant that something had gone right, though. Long distance can work. You guys proved that."

Max let out a rueful huff. "Yeah, right up until I broke up with her."

Shoving him, Brandon snorted. "Nice. Except you didn't break up with her *because* of the long distance, right? Relationships are hard, for sure, but with the right person, long distance can turn into something long-lasting."

I hate that what he's saying makes sense. I hate that every time I'm in the same room with Ava, I can't seem to think straight. It's making me so confused.

Trying to sort his muddled thoughts, Max looked back over at Ava. "Yeah, maybe. I get what you're saying."

"So... ?"

Max swung his head back sharply. "So what? It's not like I'm about to go straight across to her, wrap my arms around her and beg her to go out with me."

"Well, since you're already on a date, I don't think you need to ask her that."

Brandon's grin was back, but Max only rolled his eyes. "Come on. This isn't a date."

"You sure about that?"

"Yes, I'm sure."

"And you're one hundred percent sure that *she* sees it that way? You know that you asked her to come to a Christmas party with you, right? Just you and her."

Max stopped himself from flinging back a sharp response, finding something beginning to prod at his heart, forcing it into a faster rhythm. Yes, he *had* asked her to the Christmas party, but that had been a spur-of-the-moment thought. But his heart, he knew, wanted to share this with her.

"Wait." A thought slammed into his mind. "Do you think that *she* thinks this is a date?"

Brandon laughed and slapped one hand on Max's shoulder. "The right person to ask about that is standing over there." Tilting his chin in Ava's direction, he laughed, grinned, and then waved when Ava looked over at them both – and Max caught the flickering frown that pulled at her forehead, which was quickly followed by a slightly unsure smile.

"Quit it, Brandon." Turning sharply, Max grabbed Brandon's attention, suddenly serious. "I'm telling you the truth when I'm saying I don't know what's going on with me. I'm not sure about anything, and right now, you joking about this isn't helping." The Christmas music that tinkled along in the background seemed to add a cheery note to his words, but Brandon's smile drifted away until that seriousness was back as he gave Max a small nod.

"Sure. I'm sorry."

Max closed his eyes briefly. "I should be apologizing. I'm all out of sorts right now." *And I've got Ava to blame for that.*

"Well, you'd better step on it." Lifting one eyebrow, he spread out both hands. "She's not going to be here for much longer. If you haven't sorted out how you're feeling soon, then you're not going to get a chance."

Max shook his head, picking up his glass of eggnog. It wasn't his favorite, but he was at a Christmas party, and it felt like the right thing to be drinking. Brandon was right – the thought of her leaving without him having a chance to talk about whatever was going on with him set such a heavy weight on his shoulders that he grimaced.

"Listen, Max." Putting one hand on Max's shoulder, Brandon gave him a grin. "I'll stop teasing you about her, I swear. Go and enjoy the party – in fact, go spend time with Ava. The last thing you should be doing right now is hanging back. You want to figure out what's going on with you, then go get to know her."

He turned away, leaving Max to sip his eggnog, only vaguely listening to the Christmas tunes. It had changed from "Holly Jolly Christmas" to "I Saw Mommy Kissing Santa Claus" – and suddenly, all Max could think about was whether or not there was mistletoe hanging in the house somewhere. If he could find it, then maybe he could *accidentally* walk underneath it with her. That would make sure he'd get to plant a kiss on her before the night was out.

Sighing, Max took another sip of his eggnog. *I'm going from telling Brandon that I don't feel anything for Ava to wanting to kiss her.*

With Brandon's advice ringing in his ears, Max made his way across the room to where Ava was talking. She seemed to hit it off with almost everyone she met, which meant, Max realized, that their frosty beginning had been because of him.

"Oh no!" Someone laughed as Max approached. "Looks like Max isn't too happy."

Recognizing one of his friends, Max held up both hands in defense, taking a small step back. "Was it something I did?"

His friend, Sarah, jabbed him with her elbow as Ava smiled, watching the interaction. "You just look like you've got a heavy cloud hanging over you," she said quietly. "Walking over here with that look on your face – are you worried that Santa won't bring you anything this year?"

Max dropped his hands, aware that embarrassment was beginning to climb up his chest as everyone laughed.

Probably best just to be honest.

"The truth is," he admitted, looking over at Ava again, "seeing how great Ava was getting on with all of you made me think back to when *we* first met." He shrugged, and Ava immediately began to laugh, prompting a flurry of questions from everyone else. "I don't mind admitting that I was the grump that day. In fact, I think I've been the grump for a long time."

Sarah laughed and put a friendly arm around his shoulders. "Don't worry. You've got a good reason to be the grump, I guess. But hey, you've got all of us now – and Ava too."

Max smiled, seeing Ava's cheeks light up as her gaze danced around the group before finally landing on his.

"Although you're going to have to tell us what Max means about him being a grump," someone else said. "I'm sure that's a story worth telling."

Max's eyes widened, looking at Ava and expecting her to launch into the story, a little surprised when she shook her head.

"No, it's okay." Ava blushed prettily, then put out one hand toward Max. "I think he's told you enough already, just by being honest like that. Besides, I don't want him to tell you the situation I got myself into when I went to Dave's in retaliation!" Rolling her eyes, she laughed as everyone immediately began to ask her questions, and Max found himself smiling.

That was considerate of her.

"Now you *have* to tell us," Sarah complained as Ava shook her head. "Was it really embarrassing?"

Ava winced, tilting her head. "Embarrassing probably isn't the right word. Let's just say that Max was the one who had to save me from some guy who thought he would like to get to know me a little better, even though I wasn't interested." Her lips pressed together for a second as she looked back at him. "I think I said to you that I could have dealt with it myself, Max," she continued, now speaking a little more quietly. "The truth is, I was way out of my depth and getting nervous. Thank you for what you did."

The warmth of feeling that flooded through Max sent his lips upward as his heart followed suit. Whatever coldness had been there, whatever ice had formed between them was now completely shattered, and instead, there was something incredible beginning to grow there, like a flower planted in a desert that only needed a drop of rain to bloom.

"Well, that sounds like Max." Another one of his friends, Pam, took Ava's attention away for a moment. "Always thinking about other people and looking to see where he can help."

Hugely uncomfortable because of the compliments rather than because of the embarrassing stories, Max shoved his hands in his pockets and lowered his head so that he didn't have to look at anyone. "It's what anyone would have done," he muttered as the jolly Christmas music suddenly turned into something soft and slow.

"I really can't stay... "

"Ooo, I love this one!" Grabbing her fiancé's hand, Sarah hurried into the middle of the room and began to dance, with the other guests moving out of the way. A few others followed after, and after a second or two, Max glanced over at Ava. She was smiling softly, her eyes on the dancing – and his heart began to catapult in his chest.

I have to take a chance.

Before he could change his mind, he shrugged and held out his hand, and she took it as though she'd just been waiting for him to ask.

Her hand was soft and warm in his, and the lightning that she sent through his chest set his hair on end. He couldn't speak, wrapping his arms gently around her waist as her hands went up to his shoulders, one slipping over a little around his neck. He didn't say a single word, just listened to the song as the words drifted around them.

"I really can't stay... I've got to go away... This evening has been so very nice."

"Have you heard any more news about this new job?" Max blurted out, seeing Ava's eyebrows lift. "Remember? You said the company might be thinking about having some sort of office here."

"Oh yeah." She laughed softly, her eyes dazzling him. "I think I only told you about that yesterday. No, I haven't heard anything yet."

Max didn't know what it was, whether it was the party, being so close to Ava, or even the song, but he couldn't stop himself from asking her more. It was as if he were desperate to find out if Ava would be going home at the end of this conference and wouldn't ever be back – or if there was a chance that her being right here in Spring Forest could be something a little more permanent. And right now, he could do with permanent. "If they offered it to you, do you think you would stay?"

Ava's tongue darted out to touch the edge of her mouth, her clear blue eyes searching through his as though perhaps he might have the answer somewhere hidden inside him. The song continued to play. "

"How can you do this thing to me?"

"I… I don't know."

"I would like it if you would stay." The song came to an end, but Max kept his hands where they were, not ready to give up holding her so close.

Ava's smile grew steadily so that it lit her eyes. "Thank you, Max. If the company does decide to go for it, then I'll let you know."

"You have to promise to tell me about your decision, too. That's the only thing I care about."

The sparkles in her eyes were like twinkling fairy lights, alive with light and hope. "When I make you my decision, I promise I'll tell you." Her head tilted just a little, her gaze drifting away. "Spring Forest has had a bigger effect on me than I thought – and I've only been here a few days."

The next song began to play. This time it was "I'll Be Home for Christmas", and thankfully, Ava seemed happy to just keep dancing. "I never expected to love Spring Forest this much. I feel like there's a whole lot more for me to explore."

"That's because there is."

The corner of her mouth lifted. "Really?" She winced and looked away. "That's a dumb question; of course there is. I've been so busy with the conference that I haven't had much time to go exploring, but I can imagine there's a whole lot more for me to see."

"And I'd love to show you," Max found himself saying, finding that he meant every word with a fervency that surprised him. "You should see it here in the springtime when everything begins to get so fresh and green – and then in the summertime: Everyone here heads to the lake."

Her eyes widened. "There's a lake?"

He laughed, finding himself tugging her even closer, her body brushing lightly against his. He could feel her warmth against him, and his heart began to race. It was hard to keep his voice casual. "Sure is. In fact, there's more than one. Maybe I could show you sometime."

Her fingers brushed the hair at the back of his neck, and in that second, everything in him seemed to come alive. His breathing was shallow, his hands tightening around her waist as everyone else began to melt away. There wasn't anyone else in the room, not to him. Even the music seemed to fade. The only person in the room was Ava – and the only thing he wanted to do was kiss her.

"Wow, sorry!" Someone knocked into him, and, in an instant, he was back in the room, frustrated beyond words. It was only then that he realized that the music had changed, and now they were playing something incredibly upbeat – something he didn't recognize – which meant that everybody was dancing around the room, knocking him and Ava apart. He was about to apologize, only to see her laughing, turning around so that she could join in with Sarah and the others. Max watched her, putting his hands in his pockets as he stepped back toward the fire, trying to smile but finding himself flooded with disappointment that seemed to leach every single drop of happiness out of him.

If only I'd had time to find that mistletoe. But maybe there's another way to spend more time with her.

He wandered back over to Ava, pulling her aside. "Um, I've got a delivery in a bit. If you ride with me, I can show you more of the town and some of the neighborhoods."

"Oh, wow. You cater, too? A man of many talents, I see." Ava placed her beverage down on a nearby table. "I'm in. Lead the way."

They drove off toward the center of town in Max's four-door. About ten minutes later, he pulled up outside of a well-lit but old, two-story home.

Ava got out and glanced around. "Where are we? A nursing home?"

Max smirked as he pulled the tray of sandwiches, fruit, and dessert from the trunk and handed her the tray of homemade, decorated sugar cookies. "Close. A homeless shelter."

Ava's mouth opened wide. "Well, you really are a good guy, aren't you?" And she followed him inside.

Chapter Eleven

*T*his *can't be happening.*

There were only a few days left of the conference, but right now, that wasn't what was on Ava's mind. The only thing she was thinking about was Max.

She'd had a great time helping him at the homeless shelter the first time. It was encouraging to see the smiles he'd brought to the people there. Especially the kids. Since it was the holiday season, she'd gone back with him every day, bringing hot crockpots of his homemade soups. He'd even a cooked turkey with all the trimmings on another evening. Max was more than just eye candy. He was generous and caring.

Ava closed her eyes and put her hands flat on the table, rounding her shoulders and leaning her head forward as she took in one long, slow breath. The session had gone great, and everyone was heading back to their rooms or some evening entertainment, but she wasn't sure what she was going to do, especially when the only thing she wanted to do was to go find Max.

I can't let myself feel so much.

Her heart shuddered furiously as Beth began to float in the front of her mind. Her calls to Beth had become fewer and fewer as if she were afraid that her friend would know what she thought about Max. Perhaps Beth would be able to hear in her voice how Ava was beginning to feel.

"I can't be falling in love with him. That's crazy."

Taking another breath, she finally lifted her head. Looking around the empty room, she tried to let the quiet settle over her, smoothing her fractious thoughts. No peace came. Instead, all she felt was uncertainty.

Her mind went back to the Christmas party a couple of days ago. Dancing in the middle of Brandon's living room, the only thing she wanted to do was wrap her arms around his neck and pull herself close. Guilt had screamed at her not to do anything, especially since Max was Beth's ex-boyfriend, but she'd ignored those voices and stepped a little closer. Then the music changed from slow to fast, and everything stopped. Max had been close but not *too* close the rest of the night. It was like those few moments dancing together had been some sort of magical, mystical moment when they'd both been able to dream about something more between them, and when the music had stopped, that dream had faded away. When they'd walked back to the hotel, Max had been beside her, but he hadn't reached to take her hand or anything.

This means I might be the only one feeling this way.

A heavy sigh escaped her lips as she began to grab her things, pushing them into her bag. She didn't want to believe that, but there was a chance she was reading his signals all wrong. They'd seen a lot of each other the past couple of days, but it wasn't like he'd asked her out again.

"Hey, how did the session go?"

Ava spun around, hearing Max's voice and praying what she'd been thinking about wasn't written in her expression.

"Oh, hey, Max." Grabbing her bag, she slung it over her shoulder and walked toward him, thinking he'd keep the door open for her.

Max smiled, coming a little further into the room so that the door swung shut behind him. Ava sucked in a breath, her nerves suddenly swirling like butterflies.

Stop being dumb. You've been alone with him before.

But there was something different about this, something she could practically feel radiating between them. As if he'd felt it too, Max didn't come any closer, pushing his hands in his pockets and ambling around the room as if deliberately keeping his distance.

Her shoulders slumped. "Uh, yeah, the session went great."

"Only a couple more days to go, right?"

Swallowing, Ava nodded. "For the guests, at least. I'll be here for a bit longer, making sure that I have cleared everything up and gotten all the feedback forms and things like that." She licked her lips, glancing at Max and seeing the frown flickering across his forehead. Had she said something wrong?

"Right." He took in a deep breath and set his shoulders back a little. "So, got any plans tonight?"

Not understanding the reason for his frown, Ava collected a couple of stray pens and some sheets of paper off one of the nearby tables, managing not to look at him. "No. I want to do something, but I just don't know what."

"Great!"

That frown was gone, although Ava still didn't understand why it had been there in the first place. It was replaced by a broad smile, and when Ava's eyes met his, butterflies began to beat their wings in her stomach all over again.

"Maybe you'd like to spend a little time with me?"

I'd like to do more than just that. The images that flashed through Ava's head about marriage and a family were so strong she had to drop her gaze, struggling to look at him. "Sure. That sounds good." Steadying herself with one hand on the table, she pushed away those thoughts. They could get her into all sorts of trouble. "Got something in mind?

"I sure do."

When she shot a look at him, Max was grinning, but Ava quickly turned her attention back to tidying the tables, afraid he would be able to see everything she was thinking. "So, what is it?"

He chuckled. "It's a surprise. All you gotta do is dress warmly."

Something warm puddled in the pit of her stomach as she shivered lightly, her anticipation of being alone with Max already mounting. "I can do that."

"Great." Before she knew what was happening, he was beside her, one arm going around her shoulders, his head lowering to just beside her ear. "Whatever is making you look so frightened, you've got nothing to worry about, I swear. I'll keep you safe."

Every bone in her body turned to mush. All she had to do was turn her head and look into his eyes, and her lips would only be a few inches away from his. Desperate to be that close to him, she took in a shuddering breath, her heart screaming to be careful.

Remember what Beth told you about him?

She licked her lips, keeping her head where it was.

Why do I feel so strongly that she didn't tell me the truth?

"Okay, so you'll remember what I said about wrapping up warm?"

Max squeezed her shoulder gently, then stepped back as Ava closed her eyes. She had missed her chance but couldn't tell if she was relieved or frustrated.

"I sure will," she promised, fighting to keep her voice light. "Give me thirty minutes. Will I meet you at the front desk?"

"Come meet me outside," came the reply, a grin still fixed on his face. "Don't worry. I'll bring the hot chocolate."

Ava opened her mouth to ask him what he was planning, only to snap it closed again when he walked straight out of the room. It was all so mysterious and amazing at the same time. The fact that she was going to spend the evening with him had her heart jumping, but her nerves wound around it at the very same time.

What am I going to do if he tries to get close?

Passing one hand over her eyes, Ava shook her head, trying to settle her thundering heartbeat. Intuition told her that whatever happened tonight was either going to break their friendship or push them into something more. She just had to decide how she would respond when the time came.

***

"Okay, I'm ready."

Giving herself one last look in the mirror, Ava tried to smile away her nerves. She had every single bit of warm clothing on she could manage, topped with a cozy white hat with a pompom on top. Her gloves were in her pocket and a thick scarf was around her neck, the ends dangling near her waist.

"I just wonder what he's got planned."

Figuring that the only way she was going to find out was to actually go meet him, Ava took in a breath and turned to the door.

Her cell phone rang.

Afraid it was Max wondering where she had gotten to, Ava grabbed it out of her pocket without even looking.

"Hello? I'm so sorry, I'm just coming. I –"

"Ava?"

Ava closed her eyes, hearing Beth's voice on the other end. She'd been fielding calls from her the last couple of days, torn between guilt and doubt – doubt that Max was the same person Beth had described. Somewhere there was a disconnect, but right now, Ava wasn't certain where.

"Is everything okay?" Beth's voice was soft, filled with concern. "I haven't heard from you much these last few days, and I've been calling." There was a breath of silence. "You haven't returned any of my calls."

Ava bit her lip, a little exasperated at Beth's insistence. "You don't need to worry. I'm just fine." Swallowing hard and praying that she wasn't going to be late for Max, Ava opened her door. "Everything's been going great. I feel like I'm getting a handle on things."

There was a slight pause. "Okay, that's great." There still wasn't a smile in her friend's voice, but right now, Ava didn't have time to care. "I should have an official offer for you from the company real soon – probably by the end of the week."

Ava stopped dead, the door slamming closed behind her, her eyes widening. "Wait, what?"

"Yeah, I know. It's come about fast, hasn't it?"

Ava couldn't do anything but stare straight ahead. Everything seemed to be closing in on her at once, and suddenly her chest felt very tight.

"I don't think you're aware just how much of an impact the conference has had on the company," Beth continued as Ava put her other hand to her heart, trying to concentrate on breathing normally. "The social media impressions are through the roof! The authors have been emailing, telling the company how great this whole thing has been. The guest comments on social media have been fantastic, going on about how much they love it in Spring Forest. The company isn't wasting any time. They want to act quickly on this since it's been doing so well, so as I said, you should have an offer by the end of the week."

Still breathing hard, Ava closed her eyes, trying to find something to say. She couldn't tell how she felt, apart from being a little numb. "That... That would mean moving here, living here full time."

Beth laughed again, and the sound grated in her head, making Ava wince.

"It's ridiculous, isn't it? I told the company that I thought they were acting far too soon, expecting you to want to move to a small town when you've only been there for about a week, but they are pretty insistent. You know what the boss is like!"

Ava took a breath, and everything began to return to normal. She didn't have to decide right now. The offer hadn't even been sent yet, but the significance of it wasn't lost on her. She would have to give up everything she knew, everything that she loved about living and working in the city.

So why don't I feel any real sadness? Why is my heart practically leaping out of my chest?

It wasn't like she had a ton of friends back home. Everything in the city was busy, always rushing, barely stopping to catch a breath – but in Spring Forest, everything seemed to move a little more slowly. That was something she could definitely get used to. Yes, it would mean a change – a big change – but wasn't change meant to be a good thing?

"You've gone real quiet, Ava." There was another brief pause. "Are you sure you're okay? I haven't managed to speak to you properly for a while."

Not this again. "Like I said," Ava forced a smile, hoping it would push a bit of light into her voice. "I've just been busy with the conference. I know what I'm doing now, but I've definitely been busy. There's nothing wrong, I swear. You don't need to worry." Still, on the call, she hurried along to the front of the hotel, a slight nudge of worry sending a few lines across her forehead. Max would already be waiting, and she didn't want him to think she'd changed her mind. Being late was never a good thing.

"Are you going somewhere?" Beth's question stung as Ava pushed open the door that led to the reception. "Ava, please, if there's something going on that you need to tell me, then – "

Fire flared in Ava's chest. Whether it was from anger or frustration she didn't know, but she found herself snapping at her colleague, her words sharp and launching from her like arrows. "I don't know how many more times I need to say this, Beth, but I'm fine. Yes, I *am* rushing somewhere, but that's because I'm going out with a friend. My friend is here at the ho – at Spring Forest." *I shouldn't say that I met Max at the hotel. Not to Beth.* Taking another breath, she kept her voice firm. "So please stop worrying – and stop calling me and checking up on me. If I need you, I'll get in touch, okay?"

Her jaw tightened as Beth let out a long sigh, letting Ava hear the shake in it – but Ava gritted her teeth, refusing to allow any guilt to swirl through her. Beth just wouldn't take no for an answer. She wouldn't accept that what Ava said was what she meant, trying to get something out of her any way she could.

Is she really trying to be a good friend? Or is there something more going on here?

"Okay, Ava." Another sigh. "If you're sure." The quietness of Beth's voice made Ava wince but she bit back an apology, tugging it back into herself. She had nothing to apologize for.

"Great. I'll call you soon." Briskly, she hastily ended the call and shoved her phone back in her pocket. Hurrying outside, she took a moment to let the cold air cool her hot cheeks. She had to stop these random thoughts of marrying Max and bearing his children.

A wry smile brushed across her lips as she looked out across the front of the hotel grounds, trying to spot Max somewhere.

"Ava. Over here."

Her lingering frustration faded away, seeing Max wandering toward her, one hand lifted. Walking to him, she began to apologize.

"I'm sorry if I kept you waiting. I –"

"You didn't." Giving her a quick smile, he bent and kissed her cheek.

"You look great, Ava. But then again, you always do."

He turned around before he could react, leaving her wondering if he was just as surprised about what he'd done as she was. The imprint of his lips lingered on her cheek, and she resisted the urge to press her fingers there.

"Are you planning me?" The note of teasing in his voice had her blushing as she caught up with him, smiling when he pulled open the door for her.

"Where are we heading?"

He climbed in the opposite side, pulling the door shut. "Telling you would be no fun. This is a surprise, remember?"

The warmth that swirled in his eyes made her heart twist upside down as her fingers gripped the edge of her seat, as though she was doing everything she could to stop herself from falling head over heels in love with him.

Max grinned at her, one eyebrow lifting. "Ready?"

"Ready." Ava licked her lips as Max drove away from that hotel, wondering where exactly he was taking her.

***

"I sure hope you know where you're going." A slightly nervous laugh escaped her as she looked out her passenger side window into nothing but blackness. The truck lights illuminated the path ahead, but the road was barely a road, more like a dirt track.

"Sure I do." Max reached across and took her hand, squeezing it lightly. "Don't you trust me?"

Ava glanced at him. "Of course I do."

"Great." Giving her a quick look, he smiled. "You're anxious to know, huh?"

Flushing, she looked away. "Maybe. Sorry, I don't mean to be a pain."

"That's okay." Smiling, he took his eyes off the road for a second. "I thought we could go to the lake." Max's voice seemed to soften. "It's one of my favorite places. It won't be frozen yet, but it's still amazing." He shrugged. "Thought you might like to see it before you go."

Considerate and kind. Ava shook her head to herself. *Definitely not the man Beth described.* "I'm not sure I'm going. Not for long, I mean."

Max blinked. "What do you mean? You're staying in Spring Forest?"

Ava took a breath, letting the confusion inside her settle a little. "Well, I heard today that the company is going to be making me an offer by the end of the week. So I guess I've just got to wait for that email!"

"Wow." Max glanced at her again. "You mean they'll make you an offer to come and live here?"

"Yes – they want a new office out here since the conference has gone so well."

Letting out a low whistle, Max kept his gaze fixed on the road. "That's great. I mean, it's great that the conference has gone so well *and* that they want to put an office out here." There was a second of silence, and suddenly, the air in the truck felt a little thick. "Do you think you'll accept?"

Hesitating, Ava looked out of her window again. "I'm not sure yet. I won't have to give them an answer right away, but it's something I'm definitely considering."

119

"Really?"

Is that surprise or hope in his voice?

"It's not like I've been here for a very long time!" She laughed, then cringed as the sound died away. It sounded strained and awkward. "That's not to say I don't love it here, but I feel like there's so much more I need to know before I make a decision." Throwing up one hand, she let it drop to her lap. "Or maybe I need to just say yes and *then* come explore everything Spring Forest has to offer. I bet it has a ton of places I know nothing about."

Max chuckled, "For sure. How about places like this?"

Gesturing to the front of the car with one hand, Max chuckled again as Ava turned her attention back to the road. Her breath hitched as the lake came into view. It was huge, much bigger than she'd expected, with trees surrounding it on every single side and the moonlight dancing over the top of the rippling water. There was no way that she would have known this was here unless Max had shown her. This was obviously a secret, known only to the people who lived in Spring Forest.

Parking the truck, Max smiled out at the view. "Welcome to Tridale Lake."

"It's... incredible." Smiling over at him, she reached across to take his hand. "Thank you for showing it to me."

"No problem." His thumb ran over the back of her hand, and for a second, she couldn't look anywhere other than into his eyes.

"It's really still out there tonight." His voice had dropped a little lower as he let go of her hand, and Ava let out the pent-up breath she'd been holding. "Do you like it?"

Reminding herself to train her eyes back on the lake and not on the dark-haired, dark-eyed man sitting beside her, Ava tried to find the words. "I think it's unbelievably beautiful."

"You know something?" His head swiveled back towards her, his eyes catching glimpses of the moonlight as it streamed through the windshield. "That's exactly what I think."

A heady silence rushed through the truck, and Ava didn't seem to know where to look. Was he talking about the lake, or had he been talking about her?

Max grinned suddenly. "Want to get out?"

"Sure, I'd love to walk down to the shore and see it."

Tipping his head, Max's grin grew even wider. "What do you say about going out on it?"

She blinked. "Out?"

"Sure, on the boat." Laughing at her surprised expression, he reached across and grabbed her hand. "Don't tell me a city girl like you has never been on a boat before?"

Something constricted in her chest. "I've been on a few boats." Doubt danced through her words. "But I'm pretty sure those aren't the sort of boat you're talking about."

Chuckling, Max squeezed her hand. "No, probably not. What I've got in mind is in the little boat shed over there. The boat's not mine; it belongs to a friend. He said I could borrow it tonight." Letting go of her hand, Max shrugged one shoulder. "I figured it would be nice to row out to the middle of the lake. Look up at the moon. See the stars."

"Drink some hot chocolate?"

Max laughed. "Absolutely. I brought the flask with me in my bag."

This sounds so romantic. Her heart was going to go into palpitations if it beat any harder. "I love that idea."

"It's cold, though. We might not be able to be out for too long."

"Good thing I made sure to wrap up cozy," she teased, trying to calm her heart down. "You don't need to worry about me. I'll be just fine."

"Great. Then let's go!"

As she got out of the car, Ava's heart somersaulted. Max was proving to be one of the kindest, most generous people she knew. She'd only mentioned the lake once, and now he'd gone and organized all of this, just for her.

It doesn't seem like he's the same Max that Beth described to me. What if she was making things up? What if she didn't tell me the truth? Her teeth bit the edge of her lip. *But why would she do that?*

As if he'd known what she'd been thinking, Max came over to her, wrapping one arm around her shoulders, his breath fogging in the air. "Now, promise you're going to tell me if you start feeling a bit seasick." He grinned, dropping his head so that his voice was a little close to her ear. "The last thing I want is for you to start puking!"

Laughing a little nervously, molten lava beginning to roil in her core, Ava tilted her head up to him. "I don't think we need to worry about anything like that," she answered softly, aware of just how close his face was to hers, electricity zipping through her veins. "Not if you're there with me."

"You can trust me to look after you," he assured her quietly. "I promise you. You're going to enjoy every minute."

Chapter Twelve

Max loved the way that Ava's eyes were full of the moon. She was doing nothing but staring up at the dark blue montage, a few stars twinkling down at them both. But it was the moon that grabbed Max's attention – the moon reflected in her beautiful blue eyes.

He had taken a risk inviting her out here. They were completely alone, and this whole thing was almost as romantic as it got, but ever since the Christmas party, Max had done nothing but think about what he wanted. Right now, what he wanted was Ava. Sure, it might not make sense, and yes, it might cause a lot of problems when – or if – she went back to the city, but as Brandon had said, he had done long distance before and everything had gone well. Breaking up with Beth hadn't had anything to do with how far apart they'd been.

And Ava's nothing like Beth. What you see with her is what you get. She doesn't hide anything. His smile grew. *I never have to ask what she's feeling. It's right there, written on her face.*

"It's so quiet out here." Ava's voice was a whisper as if she didn't want to break the silence. Smiling quietly, Max leaned a little farther forward, the oars at either side of him. He hadn't rowed for a while, letting the little wooden rowboat float gently on the water. It was just the two of them, surrounded by water and beauty and the freezing cold. He shivered, but it wasn't from the ice in the air. It was the fact that Ava was so close to him, her lips pursed lightly, practically begging for him to kiss her as her eyes finally tilted up to meet his.

"I guess you don't get a lot of this sort of silence in the city."

Ava didn't laugh the way he'd expected. Instead, she just looked back at him, her eyes dropping to his mouth in such an obvious way that he went hot all over. "Yeah, you're right about that." She blinked slowly as if what he said had really made her think. "But I think I like it, you know? I think I prefer this."

Concentrate, Max. Listen to what she's saying.

He cleared his throat, the sound carrying across the water. "You mean you prefer the silence to the noise of the city?"

She nodded, her eyes drifting away from him again across the lake as though looking out at the water was bringing her the clarity she needed.

"I might say yes to the job here." Her voice was still low as if she were speaking to herself. "There's a whole world waiting for me here – a different one than what I'm used to. I've always thought I needed to stay in the city, that it was where I was happy, but now that I think about it, I guess I haven't tried somewhere new." Her lips curved gently. "Maybe there's a whole lot of adventure waiting for me right here."

"I should say there is." Max licked his lips, trying to figure out how to express just how much he wanted her here in Spring Forest. "Ava, I would be ecstatic if you decided to move here. That's not to say I wouldn't do long distance, but –"

Slamming his mouth shut on his last few words, Max closed his eyes and rubbed one hand down his face, realizing too late what it was he'd said. Ava blinked at him, and for the next few minutes, there was only the sound of the water lapping gently at the sides of the boat.

"Okay, so I guess you know what I've been thinking." He grinned a little wryly as she grasped his hand, her gloved fingers curling around his although her eyes were steady.

"You've been thinking about us?"

He nodded. "The truth is, I wasn't in a good place when you arrived – I think you figured that from the first time we met – but since then, just being around you has changed my whole world. I've done long distance before, and even though it didn't work out, it wasn't for the reasons that you might think."

Ava blinked, then looked away. "It's not my place to ask about why that ended. You don't need to explain it to me." Biting her lip, she glanced at him, a frown pulling at her forehead, sending gentle lines across her skin. Max said nothing, his heart suddenly beating furiously. He'd been honest about what he wanted. Now it was her turn.

"Max." Letting out a long, audible breath, Ava turned her head and reached out with her other hand so that she held both of his in both of hers. "Max," she said again, swallowing hard. "Listen, there's something I should probably talk to you about."

Max nodded but just sat there, waiting, with no clue what she wanted to say.

It's either going to be really good or really bad.

"The thing is… "

Ava froze, her eyes going wide at a sudden sound crashing through the water. Max could feel the way her fingers curled tighter around his and he managed a grin, despite his overwhelming apprehension.

"Nothing to worry about." Smiling at her, he squeezed her hands. "Nothing but a couple of fish."

"Are you sure?" Ava's eyes widened, looking all around the dark lake. "This is a really big lake. What if –" She shifted forward in her seat as if she wanted to get even closer to him as the sound came again. "Oh, Max… that doesn't sound like a couple of fish!"

Before he could react, Ava was out of her seat, and Max reeled back, grabbing onto her hands to steady himself. Ava seemed to have forgotten they were sitting in the middle of a boat because she kept moving, trying to shift to sit next to him – which wasn't going to work. Max knew the boat would become unbalanced.

"Ava!" Speaking as loudly as he could and trying to steady her at the same time as balancing the boat, Max tugged gently at her hands. "You can't move. Just sit down. I'll get us back to the –"

It was too late. The boat was wobbling side to side so fiercely that, after another second, Ava let out a scream and lurched to the side before Max could stop her. Toppling head over heels, she fell into the lake with a huge splash. The water flung itself back into the boat, and Max gasped in shock as icy water launched itself at him. To his relief, the boat didn't turn over even though it was still rocking furiously. Ava's head broke through the surface, forcing Max into action.

"Don't worry, Ava." Adrenaline forced energy and strength into his body as he grasped at her with both hands, hauling her body back up into the boat. Once he'd gotten her top half over the side, her legs still in the water, Max shifted carefully before, with sheer strength, he dragged the rest of her back into the boat. The boat rocked furiously, and for a second, Max was again afraid it would turn over

– but slowly, it began to subside. Ava lay there, gasping, and Max bent over her, lifting her head a little and wiping the hair from her eyes.

"Ava," he said urgently as her eyes slowly swiveled to meet his. Water dripped from her white pompom hat, which now clung to her head, rivulets running down her neck. She began to shiver but let out a groan, trying to push herself up. Max closed his eyes in relief. She was going to be okay.

"I'm so sorry, Max."

Helping her to sit back into her seat, Max grabbed the oars and began to haul on them, bringing the boat back to shore. The last thing Ava needed was to stay out in the cold. There was a real concern that hypothermia could set in unless he got her dry and warm as quickly as possible.

"You're going to be okay, Ava. I've got a ton of blankets in the truck and a flask full of hot chocolate." Daring a glance over his shoulder, he let out a gasp of relief. All his stuff was, somehow, miraculously still in the boat behind him.

"That was so dumb." Ava was shaking furiously, her words coming through clenched teeth, and the urgency that ran through Max set his heart beating furiously. He had to get her back to the truck as soon as he could.

Thankfully it didn't take him long to get the boat to shore. Dragging it up onto the sand, Max grabbed Ava's hand and half pulled her, half guided her out of the boat.

She can still walk okay. That's got to be a good sign.

"This isn't exactly how I wanted this evening to go, but you're going to have to take off as much as you can," he told her, relieved when she let out a weak laugh. "I'll help you, but I swear I'll make sure you're as dignified as possible."

"I don't care about that," Ava complained, managing to pull the hat from her head with one shaking hand. "I just want to be warm."

"Working on it." Giving her a quick smile, he pulled off her gloves and then unwound her scarf. When she was standing in just her vest top and leggings, Max turned his head. "Are you able to do the last bit yourself?" Grabbing the first thing that came to hand – a giant sweatshirt that he'd left in the back of his truck a while ago, he held it out to her but kept his head turned. "I've got blankets, but you should probably try and put this on. I'm afraid when it comes to clothes, it's the best I can do right now."

"I can't feel my feet." Ava's teeth were chattering so hard she could barely get the words out, and Max swiveled his head around to face her, seeing her ghostly pale in the moonlight. "I think you might have to help me."

He nodded without saying a word. Now wasn't the time to be thinking about her like that – right now, it was all about getting her warm as quickly as he could. Helping her to kick out of her sopping-wet leggings and top, he pulled his old sweatshirt over her head and then helped pull her arms through, although the sleeves dangled over her wrists. It fell to just below her hips, and Max was relieved that the worst was over.

Now I've just got to get her warmed up.

"That's perfect." Hating how she still shuddered violently, Max guided her to the front of the truck. "Get in. I'll find those blankets and bring them around."

Ava managed to get into the truck with a little help. She was moving stiffly, a testament to just how cold she was, and Max gritted his teeth, frustrated at himself for moving too slowly, taking too long to help her get warm. He probably should have gotten the engine going first and had the hot air blasting, but he'd been so busy concentrating on getting her out of her wet things that he hadn't stopped to think.

Catching himself shivering, Max strode to the back of his truck and found the pile of blankets. Some of them were a bit musty – they were used for Max and his dog whenever they went for a dip during one of their walks or if they got caught in a downpour – but they'd have to do. Striding around to his side of the truck, Max climbed in and started the engine. The hot air came on almost immediately but Ava shivered even harder, her arms wrapped around herself.

"Here you go. Let's wrap you up in these."

He put one blanket over her legs and another over her shoulders. Leaning forward, he managed to cover up her feet with a third before throwing the fourth one over her lap. The last one went around his shoulders – he'd gotten a little wet from all the water as well.

"There's nothing more I can do right now, Ava," he told her, becoming a little frantic with worry. "I mean, I have the hot chocolate, but right now, I think we should probably get you back to the hotel."

Ava shook her head. "I'm okay, Max. Give me a few minutes to warm up." Her shivering seemed just as bad as ever, but at least she was able to hold a conversation. "I'm sorry, Max. I'm so embarrassed."

He couldn't find her hand under the piles of blankets, so instead just squeezed her shoulder lightly. "You definitely shouldn't feel embarrassed, everybody falls out of a boat sometime, maybe just not into a frozen lake," he joked, trying to cheer her up.

She grinned and shook her head again – harder this time, and droplets of water flew everywhere. Immediately Max grabbed the last blanket from his back, putting it over her head and tying it back over her hair like a towel.

"I'll never forget it," Her eyes darted to his and then away again. "And just when you'd planned such a magical evening." She managed to smile, and to Max's relief, he saw that she wasn't shaking so much anymore. "I think I could do with some of that hot chocolate."

"Sure. But I still think we should head back."

Again, he caught a glimpse of a smile, and slowly, the tension in his frame began to melt away. Finding his bag, he pulled out the flask and one of the mugs. It steamed as he poured it gently, then handed the mug carefully to her. Ava had managed to disentangle her hands from the sleeves of his huge sweatshirt, reaching out for it. Her hands were still shaking, but she managed to lift them to her lips and take a long sip.

Her eyes closed.

"This is just what I need." She shivered again, but after that, the shaking seemed to subside. Her teeth weren't chattering anymore either, he realized, watching as she took another mouthful of hot chocolate and then another. "All that's missing is the marshmallows."

Max chuckled, his shoulders dropping as relief replaced the tension. "I do have some of those," he told her, reaching behind his seat to find the bag. "Maybe just eat some instead of dunking them. You could probably do with the energy right now."

Ava smiled, held her hand out for one, and then popped it into her mouth. Everything seemed to be going back to normal. She wasn't shivering or shaking, her teeth weren't chattering, and she wasn't half as pale as he'd seen her when she first fell in.

"Well, you did provide an unforgettable evening," she teased, her eyes closing, and she rested her head back against the seat. "Although I'm never going to live this down. How am I supposed to sneak into the hotel covered in blankets in just my underwear and huge sweatshirt?" Her eyes slid open, slanting toward him. "I'll give everyone the wrong impression."

A lump settled in Max's throat, and he coughed to clear it, telling himself that the idea he'd just had wasn't a good one. Now wasn't the time, he told himself, but all the same, the thought wouldn't leave him.

"You could come back to my place." The words tumbled out of him, quick and fast, as he saw her eyes flare. "I don't want – I don't mean... " Now it was his turn to close his eyes. "I don't mean anything by it, Ava. I could wash your clothes and then put them in the dryer. It might take a few hours, but at least then you'd have something to wear back to the hotel. There's a bath, too. That could warm you up properly and make sure that you're not in danger of hypothermia. You could have a good soak while I take care of everything else."

He meant every word, not looking for anything more from her, and to his relief, she smiled. "You're a good man, Max."

Looking away, he ran one hand over his hair. "I don't want you to feel uncomfortable, Ava. You know how I feel about you, but right now, all I'm thinking about is what's best for you. I swear."

Ava shifted a little in her chair. "I don't doubt it." Another smile, followed by her hand touching his. "I hope you make a good breakfast."

The air in his lungs froze as Max stared back at her, her words echoing around the truck. It was a ridiculous situation. She was covered in blankets and wearing his old sweatshirt. His hair was sticking up in every which way, and he was still feeling the edges of the adrenaline running through him – but when she leaned forward and pressed one hand to his face, he couldn't hold back.

His lips went to hers, his hand at her shoulder, curving around her neck. Her kiss was everything he'd ever dreamed of, only ten times better, searing through every inch of him. The air grew thick, heat rising as her other hand slipped around his neck, brushing at his hair and sending goosebumps all over him. Her kiss was soft and sweet, sending a restless, burning ache of desire right into his core. She was filling his head, filling his heart, taking every part of him and blurring it together until he couldn't seem to think or taste or smell or see anyone but her.

His heart was pumping furiously, driving need coursing through him. He wanted all of her, every part of her, and at the same time, he wanted to give every bit of himself back into her arms. It was moving too fast and too slow at the same time, and he fought to keep control. Ava tilted her head, deepening their kiss as her tongue swept to meet his. His whole body trembled, every muscle shaking as he battled to keep a hold of his passion. She was electric, and he didn't think he could ever have enough of her.

"So, how about that bath?"

The way she whispered against his lips had him groaning, her hot breath running across his lips as he drew back. He took in a ragged breath, all too aware of exactly what it was she was suggesting and just how much he wanted it.

"I don't want you to think that I'm taking advantage of the situation." Gritting his teeth, he forced himself to sit up a little. He couldn't seem to think straight when he was that close to her. "I'm happy to drop you back at the hotel. I'm happy to dry your clothes and then take you straight back there."

Ava laughed, leaned forward, and kissed him lightly. "I think I'm the one taking advantage of this situation, not you," she murmured, her words like melted honey pouring down his throat, sending a blazing fire into the pit of his stomach. "You suggested it, Max. I'm afraid you can't take the offer back."

"That's the last thing I want to do." His pulse was still throbbing furiously, feverish anticipation beginning to track its way downward. Shifting the truck into gear, he threw her a smile, seeing the same intense heat in her eyes. "I wonder how fast I can get us home."

Chapter Thirteen

"I'm going to be late!"

Max grinned at her. "Usually, that's my line."

Ava threw a pillow at him, her face flaming as she saw his gaze moving up and down her body as she climbed out of bed. She could tell exactly what it was he was thinking, and right now, she was thinking the very same thing.

Can't you stay longer?

Her cell phone beeped. *That would be a no.*

"I really have to go."

"Hey, don't worry." Max pushed himself languidly off the bed. "All I've got to do is throw some clothes on, and then I'll drive you to the hotel myself. We can walk in separately if you'd like."

Ava lifted her head and looked straight back at him. "No, I don't want that." Walking across the room, she bent down and kissed him lightly on the lips, feeling his arms snaking around her waist. "I've got nothing to be ashamed of." Giggling as he tried to pull her back onto the bed, she found herself melting inwardly, desperate to fall back into his arms

And then her cell phone beeped again.

She groaned. "That's my second alarm. I've *really* got to go, Max."

Sighing, he rolled his eyes at her, grinned, and then kissed her lightly as he sat up in bed, letting her get to her feet. "As I said, I'll drive you." Yawning, he stretched his arms up wide. "I've got an afternoon shift, but no reason I can't come in early. Make sure everything's okay for your Christmas party tomorrow."

"You really take responsibility, don't you?"

He grinned at her. "I sure do. I'm the head chef. I want to make sure that everything that happens in the kitchen goes like it's meant to – and I definitely don't want a mistake like what happened before to happen again." Knowing what he was referring to, Ava brushed her fingers down his cheek. This wasn't the man Beth told her about. He wasn't anything like what she'd said. He wasn't selfish, self-centered, arrogant, or even irresponsible. He was everything *but* those things.

"Nothing like that will happen again, not when they have someone like you in charge. You know I think you're great, right?" Her cell phone beeped again, and Ava let out a little shriek. "They're going to wonder where I am if I don't get there soon!" Forcing herself away from him, she hurried across the room. Her clothes were already laid out, washed and dried, and waiting for her. Somehow, among everything that had gone on last night, Max had managed to sort them for her. She smiled softly, glancing back over at him. "Thanks for these. Can we leave in five?"

With great reluctance, Max pushed himself out of bed, got up, stretched, and suddenly Ava's mouth went dry. Her clothes didn't seem to matter any longer; the conference was nothing but a vague thought.

He was gorgeous. Her eyes roved over him, remembering how she'd run her fingers over every single plane of his body, how his kisses had driven her to a precipice and then thrown her off – right back into his waiting arms. *He doesn't have to kiss me to drive me crazy. All he has to do is look at me.*

136

A slow, wolfish smile spread across his face. "Are you sure you *want* to go back to work?"

Ava laughed, aware of how a single look had sent billowing fire right through her. "If I didn't have to, then… "

Max laughed, walked across the room, and wrapped his arms around her so that her head rested on his chest. The steady thrum of his heart made her smile, and she closed her eyes. "I had a great time last night. Max." The urge to say more, to be honest with him, began to build in her chest, making her heart squeeze. *Why is this so hard? After everything we've shared, I should be able to be honest with him.* "I hope that we can see each other again." Tilting her head up to look at him, she caught the way his smile dropped and his eyes widened slightly. For a second, Ava was afraid that he would turn around and tell her that this was a one-time thing.

The next moment, his arms tightened around her. "Ava, I don't want last night to be the only night. In fact, I don't want this to be a one-week thing, either! There's a lot we have to talk about."

Relief poured through her, and she sighed happily. "I'm so glad to hear you say that. Maybe I can finish this conference and then we can talk? I've got the last two days to get through before I can get my head straight enough to talk to you."

A low chuckle wrapped around Max's chest. "Sure, I get that. I can wait a couple of days to talk – but we'll see each other tonight, right?"

Tilting her head back, Ava smiled up at him, closing her eyes as he dropped his lips to hers. "Absolutely."

***

137

Exhausted, Ava shut the door, walked into her room, and flopped back onto the bed. The whole day had gone well, and it had been so busy that she'd managed to keep Max out of her thoughts for most of it. There hadn't been a single issue to sort out, and she'd even begun to know some of the guests by name. It had been such a warm, friendly atmosphere that even the authors had begun to sit with the guests at lunch and dinner. This whole week was beginning to feel like she was here with family.

"I guess that's why I'm thinking about staying here." Murmuring to herself, her face split with a smile, her eyes closing as she thought about what had happened last night. It had been really dumb for her to get up in the boat like that, and she let out a sheepish giggle. She definitely hadn't meant to make it rock so badly, but the only thing she'd been thinking of was getting next to Max. The sound in the water had scared her so badly – except instead of getting to a safe place, she'd ended up dumping herself into the lake.

But Max had been right there.

He'd saved her, pulling her out of the water, getting her back to the truck, and making sure she was warmed up – and all of that had made her fall in love with him. She hadn't known the exact moment that had happened, but when she'd woken up this morning still wrapped in his arms, she'd looked into his face and realized that her heart belonged to him.

It was exhilarating.

She hadn't let herself think about Beth for a second, about what her friend would say or what she'd told her about Max. What Beth had said about him didn't seem to matter anymore.

In fact, if I'm thinking about leaving the city to move to Spring Forest, then it doesn't matter whether she finds out.

Taking a breath, Ava frowned, rubbing one hand over her forehead. Maybe she could keep this from Beth for a while and let her know once she was settled back in Spring Forest, but then Ava shook her head. No. She wasn't going to hide this from anyone, least of all Beth.

Sitting up, Ava exhaled a long breath. "I'm just going to have to be honest with her when the time comes." Looking at her cell phone as it rested on the bed beside her, Ava wondered for a few minutes whether she should call Beth right now and get it over with.

Getting up from the bed, she kicked off her shoes, padding about on the carpeted floor. No, it wasn't the time to tell Beth anything. Max was the only one she needed to be honest with. She *had* to tell him about Beth, about the fact that they were friends, and what Beth had said about him. Golden Book Publishing was a big company, and Max probably didn't think that Ava and Beth knew each other well, but it was time that he knew the truth. That was what she had wanted to tell him last night before she'd thrown herself into the water, and then after that, it hasn't seemed to matter as much.

I'll explain it to him tonight.

As she changed out of her slacks, her cell rang, and Ava rolled her eyes when Beth's number popped up on the screen. She really wasn't in the mood for conversation right now, at least, not with Beth.

Going to the closet, she tilted her head, wondering what to wear. Max had asked if she'd meet him for dinner – just the two of them – and she was looking forward to it. Yes, it was in the hotel, and yes, it would be in the middle of a shift on his break, but that didn't matter to Ava. Spending time with him was all she wanted.

And then after his shift... Ava smiled to herself, her stomach swirling deliciously. *Who knows what will happen?*

Her cell rang again, and glancing at it, Ava let out an exasperated breath and ignored the call. "I already talked to her today," she muttered, going to turn on the shower. "And I already said that I'd call if I needed."

By the time Ava had gotten out of the shower, dried her hair, dressed, and put on her makeup, Beth had called another four times. *Oh, no. I've been so busy running around. Beth is just trying to do her job and find out how everything is going, and here I am, ignoring her.*

Ava picked up the phone. "Beth, I'm so sorry. It's been crazy around here."

"I'm aware of that," Beth snapped, her formal tone gone. "Conferences are always busy. Hello! But in case you've forgotten Ava, we're meant to be friends. Something's wrong, and you're not telling me what it is. I'm worried about you."

"There's really no need. Seriously, Beth, everything is going so well." A pang of guilt hit her. *Everything is going so well with Max. Beth's ex. Who just broke up with her, leaving her devastated.*

"No. There's more to it. Something is not right." Beth let out a long and furious sigh that was obviously meant to press guilt into Ava's heart. "We've worked together for a long time, and you've not been taking my calls."

Should I tell her? No. It would only hurt her. Beth's wounds are too fresh. "I'm really, really, sorry. And, actually, uh, I really need to go with so much still going on. I can call you—"

The call went dead, and Ava blinked in surprise, looking down at her cell phone and then putting it back to her ear. "Beth?"

For whatever reason, Beth had ended the call abruptly, and Ava was left battling a ton of guilt that threatened to overwhelm her.

Swallowing hard, Ava opened her eyes and let go of a breath she hadn't realized she'd been holding. Beth wasn't reacting well to her hectic schedule, but now that she thought of it, the reason for that was probably because Beth was used to getting what she wanted.

And right now, I'm not giving her what she wants. I'm actually taking what she wants. Max. But he broke up with her, it's not like I stole him from her. That's what I'm sensing. She knows. But how could she know? Did she have spies in the area? Yeah, right. Get a hold of yourself, Ava. Beth is just bossy.

It wasn't a kind thought about her friend, but, Ava acknowledged, it was a realistic one. One thing she'd always noticed about Beth was that she could dig away at people until she got what she wanted, Ava included. After all, wasn't that exactly what she'd done with the conference? She'd gotten Ava to agree to go in her place.

"I suppose I should be grateful to her."

With a smile, Ava lifted her chin, set aside the call, and then made her way to the door. The last person she wanted to be thinking about right now was Beth, especially when her heart was filled to the brim with   someone   else.

Chapter Fourteen

"So, how's everything going?" Brandon grinned at him.

Max cleared his throat, shrugging as he looked away. "Fine. Why?"

Brandon laughed. "You're taking her to the Christmas fair, aren't you?"

"Yeah, I am." It was clear from the smile on Brandon's face that he knew *exactly* who Max was waiting for.

"Interesting. Not back to your place, then?"

Max shot his friend a dark look. "It's not like you to pry."

"Oh, well, you know me." The fact that Brandon's eyes were glinting told Max that he had something more to say. "Someone who stands at the front desk and sees someone who looks a lot like Ava coming back into the hotel in the very same clothes as she left in the night before... and you following after her." His eyebrow lifted. "It was yesterday, I think."

Max folded his arms across his chest. "What Ava and I... get up to is none of your business, thank you very much." All the same, he couldn't help but grin as Brandon let out a bark of laughter, slapping Max on the shoulder.

"So what now? Dinner last night and the Christmas fair tonight?"

"I think you mean dinner and a movie," Max replied, a smile still stuck to his face. "We picked a couple of Christmas movies to snuggle to." It was amazing. They'd had dinner together and talked about everything, from their careers to their favorite thing about Christmas. Then, after his shift ended, she'd come back to his place to watch a couple of Christmas movies. The first one had been her choice, "The Holiday", and the second one had been his. He'd managed to watch less than five minutes, though, before he'd become too distracted by her to concentrate. The way she draped herself across him had made his heart skitter across his chest, and the desire he'd found winding through him hadn't been something he could resist. Thankfully, Ava had been just as willing and just as eager – and they'd never gotten around to finishing his movie.

"This isn't just some fling, though," he found himself saying, suddenly worried that Brandon might think there wasn't anything serious going on. "I'm not doing this to get over Beth." He shrugged. "I'm already over her. You were right – it wasn't the long distance that killed our relationship. It was her. I can do long distance again if I find the right person."

"And you think you've found the right person?" Max nodded without hesitation. Somehow, he just knew in his heart that Ava *was* the right one for him. "I'm crazy about her, Brandon." Admitting that aloud didn't bring any embarrassment with it, more relief that he was able to tell his friend exactly how he felt. "We're going to talk at the end of the conference after everyone's left. There's a job for her here in Spring Forest if she wants it, too." A slow smile spread across his face as he thought about Ava living there. "I might not have to do long distance after all."

Brandon didn't say anything. He simply looked back and Max, taking everything in until, after a few seconds, his face split with a grin. "You sounded like me the first time I met Heather. I really hope you find the same thing with Ava. It's incredible being in love with someone who loves you back."

"I –"

Brandon chuckled. "Don't try and tell me you're not in love with her. I know the signs, and you should, too!"

Max laughed a little ruefully. "If I'm being honest, I'm just trying to work out exactly *what* I feel for Ava. It's like I'm standing in the middle of a twister, seeing everything else spinning around me."

"That sounds like love to me," Brandon laughed, only for his smile to fade. "Listen, Max, don't worry about this. Right now, the last thing you need to be doing is analyzing how you feel. If you think you're in love with her, then I say you're in love with her." Slapping Max on the shoulder, he shrugged. "And your feelings will only get bigger from here – if they're genuine, that is, and from the looks of things, I think they are. Don't hold yourself back. Let yourself believe it. Christmas is the best sort of time for these things."

Max sucked in the air, only just realizing he'd been holding his breath for a long time. Brandon had said exactly what he needed to hear. He was right. This wasn't the time to start worrying about if it was too soon or too much. He just had to accept what he felt, tell Ava the truth, and see where things went from there.

"Yeah, you're right."

Brandon lifted an eyebrow. "I usually am." Picking up a red, fluffy Santa hat, he dropped it onto his head. "How do I look? The boss thinks we should start adding a little bit more Christmas cheer last since we're getting so close to Christmas."

Max tipped his head to the side and laughed. "Very Christmassy. So long as she doesn't start asking me to dress up as the Grinch."

"And here I thought that would suit you quite nicely." Brandon smiled. "But then again, since Ava's arrived, maybe not so much."

Rolling his eyes, Max found himself smiling, not quite ready with his usual snappy comeback. He seemed to recognize within himself how the dark loneliness and dull gloom that had shrouded his every moment was gone – and the only person to thank for that was Ava.

"Thanks, Brandon. I'll let you get back to it." Jerking his thumb to the door, he smiled. "I'm going to go wait for Ava."

"Thanks. Buy me a candy cane at the fair, will you?"

"I might." Max winked at him. "Don't know if I'll remember, not when I'm with Ava."

Brandon snorted and then made his way back to the front desk, ready to start his shift. "Oh boy, are you in trouble," he laughed. "You're head over heels for that one, aren't you?"

Max rolled his eyes but immediately found himself smiling. *So what if I am?* The smile on his face grew. *Seems to me like Ava might be the best thing that's ever happened to me.*

***

"Sorry, I'm a bit late."

"I'm getting used to it," he joked. Leaning down, he kissed her, relishing every second of being close to her. "I didn't mind waiting."

His arms went around her, his heart quickening into a furious rhythm at the very same time. A sense of peace stole over him as he looked into her eyes, feeling as though all the final few pieces of his heart were slowly being put back together now that he had her in his arms.

"I missed you today."

"I missed you." Max couldn't hold back for a second, lowering his head so that he could kiss her long and sweet. When she sighed against his lips, he forced himself to pull back, his desire already at boiling point.

"If we don't stop, we're never going to get to this Christmas fair!"

She laughed, disentangled herself, and took his hand. "I guess we'd better get going, then."

***

The Christmas fair was wonderful. They strolled through every part of town, sampling almost everything on offer as the first few flakes of snow began to fall. Max kept Ava close, either with one hand around her waist or her fingers laced through his. The town had outdone itself. There were fairy lights everywhere with a few fire pits dotted around, ready for people to toast marshmallows. One huge Christmas tree in the middle of the town square surveyed them all; the air filled with scents of cinnamon and chocolate.

And I get to spend this evening with her.

Max smiled, one arm going around Ava's shoulders. This was the happiest he'd been in months, and Ava was the one to thank for it. When she dropped her head against his shoulder, his heart catapulted itself across his chest. This was what he wanted, he realized. This was *everything* he wanted. The hurt Beth had caused nothing more than a memory now.

"This has been amazing. Ava tilted her head toward him, the fairy lights reflected in her eyes as they stood in front of the snow-dusted Spring Forest Christmas tree.

"I'm really glad you've enjoyed it."

"I've loved every minute," she replied, laughing up at him. "I love it here." Her smile suddenly began to fade, although a softness lingered in her eyes. "If this is what Christmas is like, I can't wait to see it in spring."

Everything inside him seemed to turn over at once, forcing him to swallow hard. "It sounds like you've decided, then."

Ava nodded, her smile growing. "I've made my mind up. I love Spring Forest – and yes, I know maybe that's weird to say since I've only been here for a short while, but it's really made an impression. *You've* made an impression."

"Yeah, I'm pretty sure I did the first day we met."

Ava laughed as he squeezed his arm around his waist.

"That's not what I mean, and I think you know that."

Max pressed a feather kiss to her forehead. "I do. I'm so glad you came here, Ava. You might think that everything is changed for you, but I swear, you've changed everything for me, too."

Tilting back her head, Ava said nothing, her gaze dropping to his mouth as if waiting for him to kiss her. Max couldn't resist, a spark catching the minute his lips touched hers. It ran through his body, burning through to his core. It was more than just desire, more than just need.

This was love.

The awareness didn't take him by surprise. It was as if everything in him had just been waiting for him to recognize that, to see that in himself – and now that he did, all he felt was sheer, overwhelming joy.

"Ava." Wanting to say more, wanting to tell her about how he felt, Max was interrupted by a hand clamping down on her shoulder.

Frustrated, he tore his gaze away from Ava, only to see Brandon's smirking face.

"Thought I'd better say hello." He looked over to Ava, nodding. "Had a good evening?"

"It's been exceptional!" Ava gushed as Max frowned. "I've loved every minute."

"I thought you were working tonight."

Brandon grinned. "I am. Except the boss came and told me to have a couple of hours down here with Heather."

"Wow." Ava's eyes widened. "Sounds like she's a good boss."

"Yes, she is." Brandon smiled, then jerked his thumb over his left shoulder. "Listen, do you guys want to get something to eat? I know this place is full of chocolate and candy, but Heather and I were thinking –"

"That sounds great, Brandon, but I was thinking I would just go cook for Ava and myself." The urge to tell her exactly how he felt was getting so strong that Max found himself interrupting Brandon before he could finish asking the question. "I need to pick up a couple of things from the hotel, but then I thought we could go back to my place."

Ava snuggled into him. "Sounds good."

Her murmur sent a jolt right through him, and he widened his eyes at Brandon meaningfully, seeing his friend's lopsided smile. Right now, he didn't want to be with anyone but Ava. *She* was the only one he wanted to spend time with, wanted to talk to. And the fact that he'd just admitted to himself that he was in love with her made that need grow all the more.

Brandon didn't seem to mind, at least. He just smiled.

"Suit yourselves!" Brandon laughed, shrugging his shoulders. "I guess I'd better go and try to keep Heather away from those fresh-baked sugar donuts. She's already had a bag of six, and no doubt, she'll have another bag for me, too!

Max smiled back, lifting his hand in his friend's direction before turning back to Ava.

"Did you say you were going to cook for me?" Ava laughed as Max nodded.

"Absolutely. If you're hungry for something?"

She rested her head against his shoulder. "I'm filled with candy and hot chocolate, but I'm sure by the time we get back, I'll have my appetite back."

"Great. As I said, I need to grab a couple of things from the kitchen, but then we can head back to my place."

"Sounds perfect." Reaching up on tiptoe, she kissed his cheek. "Thank you for bringing me here, Max." Her smile dazzled him. "I've really had the best time."

He kissed her again. "Me too. I come to this Christmas fair every year, but this is the best one yet. I suppose it's only because it snowed this year," he chuckled.

Catching his sarcasm, she giggled and nudged him. Ava leaned into him, his arm sliding back around her waist as together they started to walk back toward the hotel.

***

"Got everything?"

Max grinned. "Not quite." Making his way across the kitchen and back to her, he lowered his head and kissed her long and hard, capturing the sigh that broke from her. When he pulled away, her eyes were still closed, her smile gentle.

"Wow."

Laughing softly, he went to kiss her again, but this time, Ava took a small step back, her eyes opening to look straight at him.

She wasn't smiling.

"Is there something wrong?" Worry began to wind its way around his heart as Ava quickly shook her head.

"No, there's nothing wrong. I love this. I love *us*. I know we promised we'd talk once the conference ended, but I think there's something you should know before then."

His desire slowly began to cool as Ava leaned into him for a moment, a sigh running from her. "I mean, it's nothing serious." Her eyes were screwed closed for a second. "I mean, I don't think it is, but I probably should have explained a couple of things to you before now. I guess I was afraid about how I was feeling. I never expected... " Her eyes fixed on his. "I never expected *this*, Max."

A soft smile touched the edge of his mouth, chasing away his worry. "I know exactly how you feel," he promised her. "This is all really new to me, but I'm really glad it happened."

"Me too." Ava hesitated, her gaze suddenly flitting about his face. "You know the company I work for, Golden Book Publishing? I'm guessing you know it's a big company."

Max nodded. "Yeah, I know."

"Okay, so the thing is, I –"

Before she could say anything, the kitchen door swung open. Max opened his mouth, about to bark out his frustrations, only for the words to stick to the roof of his mouth.

It was Beth.

Ava stiffened in his arms, and Mark dropped them from her waist. Beth stood framed in the doorway, her eyes wide as she stared at them. The tension grew, and Max's chest constricted, his heart painfully slamming against his ribs over and over again.

"Beth."

His voice wasn't full of confidence like he wanted it to be. Instead, it was rasping, pulling out of him from some dark place. He had never wanted to see her again, so what was she doing standing in the middle of his kitchen?

"So *this* is why you wouldn't take my calls."

Max blinked, about to snap that he hadn't been getting *any* calls from her, only to realize that Beth wasn't looking at him. Instead, she was looking straight at Ava.

With eyes that flared white, he looked down at Ava, seeing her arms cross over her chest, her foot tapping on the floor.

"I didn't take your calls, Beth, because I was able to do this conference on my own." Ava's voice was a little higher pitched than normal, obviously as surprised as he was to see Beth here.

Max closed his eyes briefly, suddenly understanding what Ava had wanted to tell him. Anger began to bubble in the pit of his stomach, spreading white-hot streaks through his veins. If Ava knew Beth, then no doubt Beth had told her something about him, and he didn't think that *something* would be any good.

"What are you doing here?" Ignoring the exchange between Beth and Ava for the moment, Max took a step forward. "You told me you'd never come back."

151

Beth pouted and stuck one hand on her hip. "In case you haven't figured it out, Max, Ava and I work for the same company. I came here because I was concerned that something wasn't going well." She rolled her eyes. "Turns out something was going a little *too* well."

I wish I'd thought of this before. Of course, Max knew that Ava and Beth worked for the same company, but Golden Book Publishing was huge. He'd never thought about whether they knew each other, and even if they had, he'd assumed it was only in a professional capacity.

"You don't need to be like that." Ava moved closer, stepping between Max and Beth. "Like I said, I –"

"You see, Max," Beth continued quickly, completely ignoring Ava. "I've been calling Ava every day, at least once or twice a day, in fact. And then, all of a sudden, she stopped taking my calls. I kept asking her if something was wrong, but she always said no and that she was fine. But I knew. I knew something was going on that she didn't want me to know about. I was worried about it all. I was worried about the conference. I was worried about the company. So I figured that if she was not going to tell me, then I would have to come here myself to see what's going on." Cocking her head, her eyes swiveled toward Ava. "Now that I'm here, I think I understand what's been going on."

Chapter Fifteen

It was like she'd gotten something stuck in her throat. The way Beth had just dismissed her, the way she was busy talking to Max made Ava feel like dirt in Beth's shoes. Easily dismissed, easily forgotten. And accused of doing something wrong.

Except I didn't steal him. He broke up with her. He's free game. She doesn't own him. And why did he break up with her, anyway? He must have had a good reason.

Swallowing hard, she lifted her chin. "I don't think that I'm the one who needs to explain anything, Beth. What you told me about Max is –"

"I never said anything!" The look on Beth's face was something between a snarl and a smirk. The dark, hazel eyes that had been fixed on Max now turned to her. There was a sharpness there, like lightning bolts being flung solely in her direction, and Ava shrank back inwardly. She could have dealt with all of this back in the city when she'd planned to sit Beth down and talk to her about what had happened, but right now, this was all sorts of confusion. Ava didn't know how to respond, how to react – and she didn't dare look at Max.

"So you two know each other." Max's hard tones rolled the words out, one after the other. Ava clasped her hands in front of her, her fingers twirling as she dared to look at him. There was thunder in his expression. His eyes seemed darker than ever before, with deep shadows underneath. His jaw is tight, his mouth pulled thin into a furious line.

Say something. Say anything! Her eyes squeezed closed. *Why didn't I just tell him all of this from the start?* She opened her mouth to tell him that she and Beth weren't just colleagues but friends – not very close friends, but friends all the same – but Beth interrupted her yet again.

"Oh, we don't just know each other, Max. Ava knows *all* about you. She's one of my closest friends," she said with an eerie stare.

"Wait, what?" Ava tried to interrupt, looking from Beth to Max, but Beth wasn't finished.

"We talked a lot about Spring Forest and everything that went on between us."

Ava closed her eyes, seeing that it was pointless to try and get a word in – but not before she caught Max's eyebrows reaching toward his hairline.

"Oh, and it seems like she didn't tell you," Beth went on as Ava's shame began to mount. "Looks like there's two of us that Ava's hidden things from. Something you're beginning to make a habit of, maybe?"

Breathing hard, Ava opened her eyes and fixed them on Beth. "Stop, Beth. Not all of that is true." Her voice was thin, guilt settling heavily on her shoulders. "You're saying – "

"You're going to stand here and tell Max that you *didn't* know about him?" Beth's voice rang around the kitchen, breaking over Ava's. "That I *didn't* talk to you about our breakup?"

"Ava?"

It was Max's quiet voice that broke her. Dropping her shoulders, she looked up at Max, aware of the darkness still written into his expression. Her excuses would mean nothing. She could tell Max that she had Beth had been nowhere *near* best friends, but what would that matter? The only thing he would want to know would be whether Ava had known about him before she'd come to Spring Forest.

She took a breath.

"You're right." Lifting her chin, she looked back at her colleague. "I didn't tell you *or* Max. First of all, I didn't tell Max about what *you'd* said about him because I didn't think he would ever be anything between us."

"Because of what Beth told you about me." Max folded his arms over his chest. "Because you believed her."

Ava flung her hands in the air. "Of *course* I believed her. She's my friend – not my close friend, no matter what she says, but all the same, why wouldn't I take her word for it?"

The darkness in his expression seemed to grow. "I don't know." Max took a step closer, now gesturing furiously with his hands. "Maybe because there are two sides to every story. Maybe because you could have *asked* me why I broke things off with Beth?" His voice grew louder. "You could have told me the truth!"

"That'swhat I was trying to do!" Finding her own temper flaring, Ava took a deep breath, barely reining in her emotions. "But I'm guessing that, even if I'd asked, you probably wouldn't have *wanted* me to know why you broke up with Beth. You wouldn't want me to hear the truth, right? The truth that you'd decided to live your own life, free of responsibilities, that you wanted to get on back out there to your own small-town life where you could fling your charms at anyone you wanted. Would you have really wanted me to know all of that?"

Except you don't know whether you can believe Beth any longer.

Her words descended into silence just as Ava closed her eyes, her heart twisting painfully as she realized what she'd said. "I-I didn't mean that. I mean, that's what I was told, but I haven't been sure – "

"Oh, I think you did." Max's voice was dangerously low, but his words weren't directed at Ava, turning his attention to Beth instead. "Is that really what you told her, Beth? Is that what you said about why we broke up?"

Beth laughed. "And now you're going to pretend that you didn't say those things?" she asked, a slight faltering in her voice. "You *said* you wanted to date other people."

Max exploded with fury as Ava found herself stumbling back, pressing against the counter. She had never seen Max like this, his eyes wide with anger, his hands curled into fists, his whole frame taut as his voice filled the room, pouring into every part of it, and Ava knew then that Beth's lies couldn't stand against it.

"Yes, Beth. I said I couldn't wait to date other people, but that was only because of how much you hurt me. I can't *believe* that you lied about me to Ava, although maybe that's what I should have expected. The truth is, I never really got to know you, Beth. You were always so good at putting on a façade, pretending to be this caring, loving person, but instead, all you wanted was to see how much you could get for yourself – and you would do anything you could to get it." He sliced the air with both hands, one on either side. "I hate that I fell for your selfish act."

Ava's hands curled under the counter, her eyes going from Max to Beth and back again. There was something in what Max had said that made her heart sink, realizing how little she actually knew Beth.

They'd never genuinely been friends. Sure, Ava had invited Beth to things outside of work, but Beth had always had an excuse as to why she couldn't make it – and had never done the same for Ava. It was like Ava had been the one she could talk to, lean on, and manipulate at work, but outside of that, she wasn't needed.

Her eyes closed, her heart shattering. *I should never have believed her about Max. Not even for a second.*

"I still want you, Max."

In the silence that followed Max's fury, Beth spoke entreatingly, her hands clasped together at her heart, her eyes wide and beseeching. "I made a mistake. I was hurt. That was why I said all of those things about you."

Max shook his head. "No, Beth. The reason you said all those things to Ava was that you didn't want her to know the truth. You couldn't *bear* to let her know what you'd done and give her the impression you aren't who you pretend to be."

Blinking furiously, Ava dragged air into her tight lungs, trying to understand what was going on. She realized now that Beth hadn't told her the truth about Max, but exactly what had caused the breakup, she didn't know.

"I never wanted to get back with Daniel, not really." Beth's voice was softer still, almost pleading with Max to reconsider. "I was afraid. I was scared about how serious things were getting between us."

A harsh laugh ripped from Max's throat. "Then you should have talked to me about it instead of texting and flirting with your ex-boyfriend. I saw your messages, Beth. I know you were arranging to meet up with him in the city – and that's when I realized what I was to you. You liked the long distance because it suited you to have more than one guy vying for your attention." He snorted. "I bet it made you feel real good."

The gasp that escaped from Ava was loud enough that Max and Beth swung their attention to her as if they'd forgotten she was standing right there. Ava's eyes widened as she stared at her friend, waiting for Beth to defend herself, to say that what Max had thrown at her was wrong, but Beth said nothing.

"I can't believe this!" She closed her eyes, one hand in a fist rubbing at them hard. "This isn't... I can't... "

"What can't you believe?" Beth asked, rolling her eyes as though Ava was the problem. "Are you surprised I didn't tell you the truth about why Max and I broke up? I was embarrassed, okay? I was hurt. That's all."

Ava shook her head. "You said things about him that weren't true." Protesting, Ava dropped her hands from her eyes. "I came here thinking that Max was the most selfish, arrogant man on this side of the state! And it turns out that the whole time, you fed me lies to cover up what it was you'd done."

Beth threw up her hands. "It wasn't serious!"

"It was serious to me." Max's voice had dropped lower still, his arms folding over his chest as though he was trying to shield his heart. "I thought about proposing. And then I found out what you were doing. You never really loved me, Beth. The only person you care about is yourself."

Ava's heart sank, seeing the flash of pain in Max's eyes. Had he really been about to propose to Beth, only to find out that she was texting her ex-boyfriend? She couldn't imagine how much that must have hurt.

"Beth?"

In answer, Beth dropped her hands, shrugged, and opened her mouth to say something, only to look away. Her expression was one of deep sorrow, her eyes glistening, her lips trembling – but Max seemed to take very little notice.

"This is over," he continued, a heaviness settling over his frame that dropped his shoulders, his steps heavy as he moved forward. "There will never be anything between us ever again, Beth. I've done a great job forgetting about you and what you did to me. You can make as many excuses as you like, or tell me that you made a mistake and you want me back – but I won't believe a word of it."

Ava closed her eyes. There was a growing ache in her throat, and she didn't think she could trust her voice, but she also didn't want Max to just leave, not when she had so much to say. Not when she had so much to apologize for.

"I'm going home." Max glanced toward her as she opened her eyes. "I guess I'll see you around, Ava."

"Max, wait." Stumbling forward, she reached for his hand, but Max pulled it away, and all she touched was air.

"Not now, Ava." His voice was brusque, and with a shake of his head, he walked straight out of the door, leaving Ava's heart in pieces.

The minute the door closed behind him, Beth rounded on her.

"I can't believe you tried to start something with my boyfriend!" The sadness that had been on Beth's face only a few seconds ago was gone in an instant, replaced instead with a fit of furious anger.

Her eyes were narrowing, spitting fire, and one finger pointed accusingly in Ava's direction.

"I didn't *try* to start anything." Taking in a long breath, Ava steadied herself against the force of Beth's outrage, seeing her supposed friend for the person she really was. "The more I got to know Max, the more I began to wonder if what you'd told me about him was the truth. As I got to know him, I knew what you said was wrong."

Beth shook her head, her lips curling back into a snarl. "You can't have him. I won't let you."

The wave of shock that pushed back against Ava had her shuddering violently, her hands gripping the counter again. "That's why you came," she found herself murmuring through trembling lips. "You came because you were afraid I'd met Max and realized that you hadn't told me the truth." Her head lifted as she looked into Beth's face, seeing how she took a small step back, her face beginning to pale from the red that had burned there only a few minutes before. "You don't want me to have anything to do with him because he's the one thing you haven't been able to keep, the one person you haven't been able to manipulate into giving you what you want."

"You don't know me."

"You're right," Ava shot back quickly. "We're *not* friends, Beth. You use everybody. I didn't start something with your boyfriend. I started something with your *ex*-boyfriend, who, by the way, I think is really great. He's nothing like you said. In fact, he's everything that someone like me – or someone like you – could want and more." Letting go of the counter, she took a moment, looking back into

160

Beth's face with a steadiness that surprised even herself. "I think you've realized how much you've lost in letting him go. Maybe you've finally grasped just how dumb you were in thinking that someone else would be just as good, if not better, than him."

Beth's cold, harsh laugh whipped across Ava's skin. "Looks to me like you've lost him, too."

Ava's shoulders lifted, inwardly recoiling in pain at the thought that she might never be close to Max again. "Maybe I have, but at least I can accept that it was my fault. I should never have believed you. I should've trusted my instincts about you and your character – and I'm glad I have now, even if it's too late."

Beth's hands went to her waist, her eyes flashing. "And what sort of person am I, then?"

I'm really not in the mood for this.

She began to walk to the door. "I didn't see it until right now, Beth. I've had my doubts, and I've questioned a lot of things – things I should have questioned sooner. You never ask me about my life because you're too busy telling me about yours. If you've got a problem, then you'll find someone to solve it so that you won't have to deal with it. *You* should have been the one back here at Spring Forest for the conference. It wasn't about Max, it was about *you*. You played the emotional card, making me feel sorry for you when you just didn't want to show up back here because of how ashamed you were about the breakup. All of the stuff you told me about feeling hurt and how much you couldn't bear to see Max again was nothing but lies." With one hand on the door, Ava looked over her shoulder, her vision suddenly blurring. "I'm glad I've learned the truth about all of this. I only wish I'd been honest with Max from the beginning."

Before a tear could fall, Ava pushed open the door, only for a sudden thought to slam into her mind. Turning her head, she looked back at Beth, who was standing with her hands by her sides, looking a little lost. "Oh, and by the way, I think I'll be taking that job here."

Turning her head, Beth slid her gaze back to her. "Why? There's no way that Max is ever going to – "

"What happens between Max and me has got nothing to do with you." A new strength filled her voice as she spoke. "Maybe this can't get sorted out, and maybe things will be really awkward for a while, but I've found something here that I didn't think I would *ever* be given: a chance to start over. A change to build my life from the ground up, find opportunities, and make new friends, and right now, that's   exactly   what   I   need."

Chapter Sixteen

Hunching his shoulders against the cold, Max walked down Main Street, away from the Christmas tree and the twinkling fairy lights. It was getting darker with every step – which matched his mood exactly. He didn't know where he was going. He just needed to get away.

He hadn't seen Ava all day. In fact, he'd deliberately gone out of his way to make sure he didn't bump into her. Keeping himself busy in the kitchen most of the day, when his shift had ended, he'd gone out to the back instead of walking through the hotel like he usually did. Sure, it had meant that he'd missed out on catching up with Brandon like he usually did, but right now, he didn't feel like talking to anyone.

I just hope that Beth's gone back to the city.

Even now, the memory of her stepping into the kitchen made him wince. He hadn't been able to breathe when he saw her in the doorway. Everything he'd left behind had come to pour itself over him again, and he'd felt the weight of it all – the upset, the heartbreak, the regret, the pain. It had all pierced through him.

The first flakes of snow began to fall from the sky, but Max didn't look up. Instead, he shoved his hands in his pockets and just kept walking, head down, feet stepping one after the other, trying to make sense of it all.

Ava should have told me.

That was the worst part. Knowing what he felt for Ava, the fact that she hadn't said anything about Beth before now hit him like a truck, and then some of the things she'd said last night, well, that had been hard to hear. Even though she'd tried to take it back, even though she'd tried to apologize and explain, he still felt it all.

Shaking his head, he huffed out a breath, seeing it frost the air. For a while there, he'd been excited about Christmas, looking forward to the holidays and what was in store. It was as though what he'd found with Ava had been one great big gift, just needing to be explored, and now everything seemed very dull again. The Christmas lights didn't hold any sparkle. Not for him. Not anymore.

The snow began to come down a little heavier, and Max scowled, turning up his collar against it. Glancing around to see where he was, he caught sight of Dave's but shook his head. Sitting in there would only remind him of being with Ava, of what had happened the last time he'd been in there with her. He had too much going on in his head to think about that now.

A wry, sad smile curved the side of his mouth. *Although I guess this explains why she was so cold to me at the beginning.*

"Max."

Jerking his head around, his brow furrowed at the sight of Brandon hurrying down the street toward him, calling his name for the second time. A little irritated, Max lifted his shoulders, keeping his hands stuck in his pockets.

"What?"

"I've been calling your cell." Breathing hard, Brandon sucked in the air. "I know it's not your shift, but there's been some sort of disaster in the kitchen. And with that Christmas party about to start –
"

"Whatever's happened, they're going to have to deal with it without me," Max spoke tightly, interrupting Brandon. "Seriously, man, I don't want to go back to the hotel tonight."

Brandon took a second before he spoke, surprise written across his features. "Why? That's not like you. You know how much this Christmas party means to Ava as well, don't you? It's the last night of her conference."

Max shrugged. "I'm sure the kitchen team can handle it without me."

"Yeah, and sometimes they need you. Heather's desperate for your help. Do I really need to remind you that you're the head chef?"

"Even the head chef needs a break sometimes."

The silence grew between them for a few seconds as Max scowled, feeling the shock bouncing off Brandon. His conscience was trying its best to battle against his will, but it wasn't managing to even pierce it.

"What's going on, Max?" Holding out his hands to the side, Brandon held Max's gaze, forcing him to look at him. "This isn't the Max I know. You've never said 'no' to something like this. You're *known* for being someone people can rely on. You always take such pride in your work, in the hotel – and the hotel needs you right now."

Max pinched the bridge of his nose as large white flakes continued to fall silently around them. "Brandon, I really can't do this right now."

"Why not?" Grabbing Max's arm for a second, Brandon moved a little closer. "Is it something to do with you and Ava?"

"I don't need to share everything with you, Brandon." Aware that he was snapping for no good reason, Max jerked his arm away. None of his anger was directed at his friend, but it was coming out all the same. "Stop prying."

"And you think that's what I'm doing?" Brandon snorted. "Seriously, Max. We're best friends."

"We *are* friends." Max began, but Brandon wasn't finished.

"In case you haven't realized, *you* were the one who didn't tell me about Beth. *You* were the one who didn't tell me how much she meant to you *or* that you were planning to propose. Then after you broke up, you kept a lot to yourself, bottling it all up until it began to eat away at the heart of you. If I'm your friend, then I'm here to support you." He shrugged. "That's all I'm trying to do here. I'm not asking you about what's happened between you and Ava because I want you back working at the hotel tonight," he continued, as though he could tell what Max was thinking. "I'm asking because I don't recognize my friend right now." Shrugging, he began to turn away. "Let me know when you want to talk. I'll be here to listen."

Letting out a breath through clenched teeth, Max scowled after Brandon, watching him turn around and walk back up the street. Trying not to let anything his friend had said pierce his heart, he swung back around, striding down the street in the opposite direction, his footsteps heavy and weighted.

What does Brandon know? He's got Heather. He doesn't have any problems.

His gut twisted.

But that doesn't mean he won't understand.

Max let out a hiss of breath, his conscience finally winning over. Brandon was right; he *was* being a jerk right now, lost in his own dark sea, oblivious to everyone else around him. Didn't Ava mean more to him than that? This was *her* Christmas party, the last night of the conference – and if there was a disaster in the kitchen, then that might affect what happened at her party.

"I don't want that for her." Closing his eyes and aware of the sting of his pride, Max puffed out another breath and turned around.

"Brandon."

It took a couple of shouts for Brandon to hear him, but after a moment, he stopped and waited for Max to catch up.

"Okay, I'll come to the hotel."

Brandon nodded but didn't say a word.

"And – and you're right," Max said before he'd even really decided that he was going to say something about Ava. "Something did happen. Beth showed up."

Brandon's expression didn't change, and Max grasped his friend's arm, stopping for a second.

"Wait, you knew she was here?"

"Of course I did. I work the front desk, remember?"

"If you knew, then why didn't you tell me?"

Brandon gave him a small shrug. "It's not my place to ask, but then I figured that something must have gone real bad, the way you've kind of retreated back into yourself a little bit."

"Thanks." Letting out a groan, Max rubbed one hand down his face. "It was all such a disaster. I've been so dumb. It never occurred to me that Beth and Ava would be friends. Golden Book Publishing is a big company, so I figured they might just know each other professionally."

"Okay, but why is that such a bad thing?"

"Because Ava didn't tell me." Something exploded in Max's chest as he spoke. "She should have said she was friends with Beth from the beginning. Beth said last night that she and Ava were really close friends; I'm not sure that's true, but she should have told me much sooner than this."

Max didn't expect to hear a laugh flying from Brandon's lips. He stopped dead, staring at his friend as snow continued to fall.

"I don't get what's so funny."

Brandon shook his head and ran one hand over his chin, still grinning as though Max should be able to work it out himself. "Do you really think in the scenario you've just laid out that anything would have happened between you and Ava? If she'd told you that she was friends with Beth, I guarantee you wouldn't have gone near her. In fact, you'd probably have made an effort to stay as far away from her as you could."

Max grimaced. "You can't know that."

"Yeah, I can." Brandon's eyebrows lifted. "If you're honest with yourself, I think that's exactly what you would have done – and nobody would have blamed you for it. After everything that happened with Beth, the last person you'd want to hang around with is one of her friends."

Max chewed on his bottom lip as he began to walk again. "I don't know." Shrugging, he turned his head away, his brow furrowed. "Maybe I'd have gotten to know her."

"I doubt that."

Again came that niggle of conscience that Max knew he couldn't escape from. His friend was right. If Ava had told him the truth from the beginning, then he wouldn't have gone near her. He just hasn't even wanted to admit that out loud.

"I can tell you that Ava is the best thing that's ever happened to you, even if you can't see that right now." His friend gave him a nudge as they walked up to the hotel. "She's a better fit for you than Beth ever was."

Max sighed heavily, a little of the pain and confusion beginning to fade. "I know that."

"Then the question is," Brandon continued as they stepped into the foyer. "What exactly are you going to do about it?"

***

When Max had walked into the kitchen two hours earlier, he'd instantly been grateful for his firefighter training. Heather had been dealing with a server who seemed to have catapulted himself across the floor while, at the same time, something had burst into flames in the corner of the kitchen. The stand-in-line cook had not shown up for work which had left Heather understaffed. Now, hours later, they finally seemed to have everything under control.

"Thank you, Max." Coming toward him, Heather spread out both hands. "I don't know what we would have done without you."

Max winced, having almost been about to say that he'd been happy to help, but instead, he looked at Heather and shook his head.

"Max?"

"You can thank Brandon for getting me back here tonight."

"Wait." Heather's eyes flared as she put one hand on his arm. "If I'd known you were busy, then –"

"I wasn't busy. I was being selfish." Max shrugged as Heather frowned. "Brandon gave me what I needed to get some perspective."

The smile suddenly fled from Heather's face. "Wait, this is because of Beth, isn't it?

Max was not surprised that Heather already knew his ex-girlfriend was in town. They'd all gone on double dates before Max and Beth had broken up, so it wasn't like she didn't know who Beth was.

"Yeah, she appeared last night out of nowhere."

"And now she's gone back to the city," Heather added, with a slight lift of her eyebrows. "Looks to me like she didn't get what she wanted."

Blinking, Max let the moment of surprise pass. "I don't think she wanted me."

"I wouldn't be so sure about that." Heather shrugged. "Maybe she realized what she's lost. Regret has a way of doing that to people. "

"She never had a chance." Max's thoughts immediately went to Ava. The last thing he wanted was to lose her. "You're right, though, about regret. I don't want to do anything that would mess things up with Ava."

"I'm sure you don't."

He smiled quietly. "I don't have any anger toward Beth anymore if I'm honest. Brandon helped me see the bigger picture. I suppose he is my best friend," he laughed, making a jabbing motion with his fist.

Then he sighed, running a hand over his face. "He's right. If I'd known Ava and Beth were friends from the beginning, then I'd have stayed a million miles away from her. Look what I might have lost."

Laughing, Heather playfully nudged him. "I don't think it's me that you need to be saying all this to." With a look toward the door, she laughed again as he grinned. "I'll take care of the rest here. Go on. Go and find her."

Max   didn't   need   to   be   told   twice.

Chapter Seventeen

The smile on Ava's face wasn't genuine. She'd plastered it there at the start of the Christmas party and had kept it fixed for the rest of the night. The Christmas party was meant to be the big event that ended the conference, but right now, all she wanted to do was head up to her room and curl up in bed.

"This has been such a great night!"

"I'm so glad you enjoyed it." Reminding herself to always be professional, Ava stood a little taller, straightening her shoulders. "And I do hope you'll consider coming back. I know that the attendees have loved having you here, and I can guarantee they'd be thrilled if you come again next year. Golden Book Publishing would be delighted as well."

Clayton Scott – the horror author, Ava silently reminded herself – let out a broad laugh that had a slight huskiness to it. "Ava, you don't even have to ask! I've already sent my request for next year's dates to my agent to send to the company. Is that going to be the *only* conference next year? I've heard rumors that there might be something else happening next year before Christmas, and I'm eager to hear about anything new going forward."

Ava's smile grew, no longer as fixed as it had been. "That's great to hear. Yes, the rumors are true – there might be some new things coming up for the company right here in Spring Forest."

"That's excellent news." Clayton grinned at her. "I've loved every minute of this conference – and that says a lot about you! You should be very proud of all you've achieved here."

Her smile dimmed a little. "Thank you. I am."

Except when it comes to Max, she thought to herself.

"Great. I look forward to seeing what you do next!"

Ava smiled, looking away. "Thank you."

Before she could try to find something else to say, someone else came over to Clayton, letting Ava slip away to the back of the room. She wasn't in the Christmas spirit. She might have done well in her professional life, but in her personal life, she had blown it.

I can't stop thinking about him.

Max hadn't been far from her thoughts, even though it was the last day of the conference. She'd managed to get through it all, but now in the quiet moments, she couldn't help but think about him. She hadn't seen him since last night, and her stomach hadn't stopped churning since, afraid now that things were over between them.

"I should have told him about Beth much sooner." Murmuring to herself, she rubbed one hand over her eyes, aware of the tears that threatened. The fact that they'd gotten so close so quickly meant that, right now, the separation was slowly killing her, driving a knife right through her spirit. This wasn't the way things were meant to end. Ava was finishing the week hiding in the shadows instead of stepping into the glitter of sparkling Christmas lights. She'd already sent the e-mail accepting the job here, but what would it be like coming back to Spring Forest now? What if Max didn't want to be around her anymore?

Her best Christmas had suddenly become the worst.

"I'm sorry to interrupt what looks like a really deep conversation with yourself, but someone is looking for you."

Ava jerked away from the wall, having not expected the voice or the tap on the shoulder. She saw Lucinda, one of the authors, smiling back at her.

"Hi, Lucinda, sorry. I was just… thinking." With a quick smile, she stood tall, trying to remind herself to get back into professional mode. "Never mind what I was thinking. Did you say that someone wants to speak to me?"

Lucinda grinned. "I'd love to hear what you were talking about with yourself. I bet I could put it into a book." Laughing, she put one hand on Ava's shoulder. "Yeah, sorry, there's someone from the hotel looking for you. I think they've gone into that little 'Winter Wonderland' you've got outside."

"Great." Excusing herself, Ava headed across the room to the French doors at the back, then pushed them open. The Winter Wonderland was a separate feature, hired from a company nearby. It didn't look like much outside – just a long, broad, rectangular tunnel of sorts – but it was spectacular from the inside. When Ava had stepped in for the first time, it felt as though she'd been walking somewhere at the North Pole.

"Hello?" As she pushed aside the thick, black drapes that hung at the entrance, hiding the start of the experience from the outside, Ava walked in, unable to stop herself from smiling. What felt and sounded like real snow crunched under her feet, and tiny flakes danced in the air around her. There was a slight nip to the air, too, but Ava barely noticed. Reindeer and woodland creatures moved around on either side of her, with what sounded like sleigh bells in the background. Moving forward, she made her way into the next part, smiling down at the floor that was painted to make it look as though she was walking across a frozen pond. Ava resisted the urge to tiptoe.

There didn't seem to be anyone else around.

Maybe whoever is looking for me went through this place already. Ava shivered lightly as the cool air brushed across her skin, lifting goosebumps as it went. To her left, a group of penguins erupted into a Christmas carol, making her jump. Rolling her eyes to herself, she paused for a second, looking at them. They were cute and certainly made her smile. Perhaps she'd be able to find a little bit of happiness this evening after all.

"Ava."

Turning around quickly, her heart tore through her chest as Max walked to her, his eyes fixed on hers. Instantly, everything in her seemed to burst into flames, and, instinctively, she pressed her hands to her cheeks, stepping back as he came closer.

"Max." Her voice was rasping. "I – "

"I'm glad I found you. I'm sorry it took me so long." That familiar soft smile was back, his lips no longer pressed into a harsh line. "Brandon and Heather talked some sense into me – sense that I should have had from the start." The way his lips smirked had her heart tumbling over itself. This was so different from how he'd been last night. This was back to the Max she knew. The Max she loved.

Relief forced her forward, looking up at him through tears. Max was waiting for her, opening his arms as she stepped into them.

"I really am sorry." Max shook his head, bending it forward. "I was afraid. Seeing Beth again made me crazy. Everything she did, all the hurt she caused, it all came back, and I reacted poorly."

"I understand that." She swallowed hard. "I should have told you about Beth before – I intended to, but then she came, and then everything went wrong."

A single tear splashed onto her cheek as the penguins began to squawk their Christmas carol all over again, making her laugh through her tears. "I didn't tell you at first because I didn't think it was important. And then when things started changing, I guess I was afraid of what would happen if I did."

Max pulled back from her a little, one hand running over his face for a second. "I get it, Ava. I get why you didn't tell me that you knew Beth."

"We're *not* best friends; I was convenient for her, it's what my heart knew all along." Suddenly afraid, she looked up at him, her eyes flaring. "I know she said, but –"

Smiling, Max lifted one hand to her face, his thumb running gently over her cheek. "Don't worry. I believe you. Last night was *my* fault. I wasn't being rational, and I definitely shouldn't have reacted that way. I'm sorry." Laughing a little ruefully, he shrugged. "I actually think it was a good thing you kept it to yourself."

Ava looked up at him, and her eyes were suddenly wide. "Really?

"Yeah, I am. As I said, Brandon made me realize that if you'd told me about Beth from the beginning, then I *definitely* wouldn't have wanted to spend any time with you." His other hand lifted to her face, their gaze melding as Ava slowly began to melt into his embrace. "I would have missed out on the best thing that's ever happened to me. *You* are the best thing, Ava. I can feel it right here."

His hand dropped, pressing to his heart, and Ava's eyes began to fill with fresh tears. He was saying all the things she had been so desperate to hear, realizing just how much she meant to him. There had been a second where they'd almost lost each other, but now, she was back in his arms – and that was the only place she wanted to be.

"I feel the same." She took a breath, closing her eyes as tears ran down her cheeks. "I love you, Max. I was so afraid that I was going to lose you. I was so angry with myself for having not told you the truth about Beth. I didn't know what to do. I was lost, sinking into the shadows and feeling like everything in my life – including my future – was slowly crumbling because you wouldn't be in it."

"But now you don't have to worry," he murmured, bending his head so that his mouth was close to hers. "Because your future is going to be right here with me." His lips brushed against hers, and electricity ran straight through her. "I love you, too."

***

One week later.

Taking a deep breath, Ava closed her eyes for a second. Brandon had already told her that Max was in the kitchen, working late. But since he didn't know she was here, Ava's tension coiled a little more.

Unable to wait for a second longer, she pushed open the door to the kitchen. She had been one whole week without Max, one whole week where she'd done nothing but missed him like crazy. One whole week where she'd imagined the moment she could step back into his arms.

"Hi, Max."

A smile flitted across her face as Max turned his head, his hands pressed flat on the counter. The way his eyes went wide, followed by his huge grin, made her giggle, and before she knew it, she was swept up into his arms.

"What are you doing here?" he laughed, twirling her around as she buried her face into his neck, breathing him in. "I didn't think you'd be coming until after Christmas."

"I couldn't stay away for so long." Ava pressed both hands to his face as he set her down gently. "My Christmas in the city was just going to be a quiet one – so why would I stay there when I had all this here? Plus," she continued, her voice softening. "I missed you."

Max's green eyes flickered. "I missed you, too." His smile grew as he lowered his head. "I missed you so much that I was thinking about coming to the city for Christmas. Looks like you beat me to it!"

Ava laughed, tilting her head to one side. "Except I'm here to stay."

Max's smile dropped into an open-mouthed circle that let out his gasp of surprise, his eyebrows tearing toward his hairline as Ava laughed again, reaching up to kiss him lightly.

"I-I don't understand." Max ran one hand through his hair. "I thought you weren't going to be moving until after New Year's."

"My company said I could move here whenever I wanted, so long as I was set up for the second week in January," she told him softly. "So I got my place in the city packed up in record time and booked my flight. I'll have to stay at the hotel for a few days until I can find a place to rent, but –"

Before she could say anything else, Max kissed her so fiercely that her breath was stolen away. She leaned back into him hungrily, only now realizing just how desperately she'd missed him.

"You're staying with me."

Ava's eyes took a second to open, Max's gruff whisper chasing down through her, right to her core. "For how long?"

Max shrugged and then grinned, his eyes twinkling. "For as long as you want." His lips hovered dangerously close to hers. "I won't be chasing you out anytime soon."

Loving his response, Ava flung her arms around his neck and let him pull her close. She sighed happily, her head resting on his shoulder as his strong arms encircled her waist.

"The only place I want to be is with you, Max," she whispered in his ear. "This Christmas has given me the only thing I think I could ever want. Your Christmas kisses have stolen my heart."

Max's answer was to kiss her again, soft and sweet, until every part of her was melting.

"You're the best present I think I could have ever asked for," he murmured against her mouth. "I'll give you Christmas kisses whenever you ask."

Ava laughed softly, her hands running through his hair as she leaned back in his arms. "Then how about right now?"

Epilogue

"No peeking. Keep your eyes shut."

Ava giggled as Max pulled open the car door. Swinging her legs out first, she waved her hands around the air blindly in front of her, just as Max's strong hands grasped hers.

"I still have no idea where we are."

"That's the point of surprises." A smile was flooding through Max's voice as Ava clung to him, threading one arm through his, her fingers tight around his wrist.

Something brushed across her cheek, and she tilted her head back, her eyes still covered with a blindfold. "Is it snowing?"

"Yep."

"I thought it might be." The sky over Spring Forest had been a threatening gray for a few days, but not a single flake of snow had fallen until now.

"Okay, we're almost there."

Ava had no idea where they were, but she was here with Max, and that was all that mattered. After almost a full year of living in Spring Forest, she had never been happier. Her relationship with Max was a like a fairytale, and their love for each other had grown so strong nothing could separate them now. Moving to Spring Forest – and in with Max – had been the right choice. It had brought her a whole different way of life and, with it, a love that she had never expected to find.

"Great, we're here." Max let go of Ava, her arm sliding out from his. Ava stopped in her tracks, not daring to take a step forward now that he was gone.

"Max?" There was a slight wobble to her voice. "Max, where are you?"

"I'm right here." His hand touched her arm and then pulled away again. "I think I'm ready." There was a breath of silence. "You can take your blindfold off now."

Aware of the slight curl of nervousness in her stomach, Ava tugged the blindfold from the back of her head, and it fell away. Blinking in confusion, she looked first around, and then at Max. "We... we're at the hotel." Her cloud of confusion grew even bigger when Max began to smile.

"Not just at the hotel, Ava." Moving closer to her, Max reached out both hands and took hers, threading her fingers through his. "This is the very spot where we met."

A very different sensation began to wind its way through Ava's frame, her eyebrows lifting gently. "Really? Right here?"

Max nodded. "Do you remember what happened?"

A spirited laugh broke through her lips. "Of course, I remember! In fact, I'll never forget," She shook her head lightly. "You were a real grouch that day. I remember that!"

Beaming, Max laughed, snowflakes coming down a little harder as they fell around them both. "Yeah, I guess I was, but I've never been able to forget that moment." His smile was slowly fading, a seriousness driving through his expression. "It was the moment when everything changed, the moment my life went in an opposite direction – a direction I've been walking in ever since. I have you to thank for all of it. You've given me so much, Ava. I don't think you'll ever know how much."

"I feel the same way." Squeezing his fingers, Ava tilted her head slightly. "I never thought I'd move to a quiet town like Spring Forest, but this is the happiest I've ever been in my whole life. I love living here with you, Max. I love this little town. I love everything about my life here – and I love you."

"I love you, too." Dragging in a deep breath, Max pressed his lips hard together as Ava's heart began to thud furiously. "I wanted to bring you back to the same spot where we met so that I could ask you something. Something I've wanted to ask you for a while." Without missing a beat, Max let go of one of her hands and dropped to one knee, tugging a small, red, velvet-covered box from his pocket. His head lifted, an intensity searing through his gaze. "Ava, my darling," He took another breath. "Will you marry me?"

It was as if the snow clouds had parted, and brilliant sunshine was pouring down through the sky toward her. Ava couldn't speak, her throat constricting, her hands flying to her mouth as she stared down at the beautiful diamond ring held up to her. Max licked his lips, waiting for her answer, as Ava stood there with her mouth gaping wide open, suddenly speechless.

Eventually, Max broke the silence.

"Ava?"

Her hands dropped excitedly to her sides.

"Yes!" she yelled enthusiastically.

In a split second, Max had lifted her off her feet, pulling her into his arms and hugging her so tight, never wanting to let her go.

"I love you, Ava." Max's whisper softly tickled her ear. "I love you so much."

She wrapped her arms around his neck, half laughing, half crying, as she pulled herself as close to him as she could get. "I love you, too."

The air filled with whoops and cheers, and as Max finally released her a little, Ava saw that a crowd of her friends had turned up, rushing toward them as Max finally set her down.

"I had them watching from the hotel lobby," Max winked, lifting her chin with one finger as he looked down into her eyes. "I wanted them to be here to share this moment with us. I didn't want you to ever forget it."

"I don't think I ever will. Although this doesn't replace your grumpy first impression, buddy." She joked, her vision blurring with tears. Ava kissed Max long and hard, surrounded by the cheering of her friends. Nothing but joy flowed around them, her heart overflowing with love for the man who held her heart.

"Here." Max took the ring from the box and held it out to her as swirling snowflakes danced around them. Giving him her hand, Ava's breath caught as he slipped the engagement ring onto her finger. Gentle tears rolled down her cheeks as she looked up at him, seeing the smile on his handsome face. "I love you, Max."

Max dropped his head and kissed her. "I love you too, Ava. I'll be counting the days until I get to marry you."

Smiling softly, Ava pressed her hand lightly to his cheek, her ring sparkling in the winter sunlight. "My heart belongs to you forever. I can't wait to be your wife."

Afterword

Thank you for reading my book, Christmas Whispers! It was a pleasure to write, Christmas is a magical holiday that I enjoy so much.

If you'd like to help me out I'd be overjoyed if you took a moment to leave a review here

"Escape to you" is a sweet, mountain town, single mom, enemies to lovers romance novel. Brent and Aubrey both experienced heavy heartache before found each other. Read this one if you like a beautiful mountain setting and characters you just can't wait to be together.

Get it here >> Escape to You

"Back to You" is a sweet, small town, second-chance romance novella. Luke and Savannah will make you laugh and cry as they rekindle their old flame years later after kids and failed marriages.

Get it here >> Back to You

"The Heart Knows Best" is a wholesome quick read beach romance. Hunter and Daisy are called to leave the busy city to save their marriage. Complete with a happily ever after, you'll fall in love with their love story.

Get it here >> The Heart Knows Best

Please follow me on Facebook for my up-and-coming books! More great ones are in the works, I truly appreciate your support!

Xx,

Jada Stone

Printed in Great Britain
by Amazon

15192829R00108